Proposal

By Meg Cabot

Proposal

A Mediator Novella

MEG CABOT

AVONIMPULSE

An Imprint of HarperCollinsPublishers

An excerpt from *Remembrance* copyright © 2016 by Meg Cabot, LLC.

EPub Edition JANUARY 2016 ISBN: 9780062473561
Print Edition ISBN: 9780062473585

Avon, Avon Impulse, and the Avon Impulse logo are trademarks of HarperCollins Publishers.

AM 10 9 8 7 6 5 4

DEAR READER,

I can't thank you enough for reading this, the first e-novella installment to a book series I created some time ago.

But don't worry if you missed any of Suze Simon's previous "progress reports." After all, they took place in high school. And who wants to relive high school?

Except that it was in high school when Suze first encountered the love of her life, Jesse de Silva. It took a miracle to bring them together, and now that they're adults, they've sworn that nothing will ever tear them apart.

Or will it?

If there's one thing I've learned since high school, it's that life is full of miracles . . . and surprises, like that a book series I wrote so long ago would have had such a lasting impact on the lives of so many, especially my own. And for that, I'll never stop being thankful.

So thank you so much for reading . . . and please keep on doing so! I promise to deliver a lot more surprises . . . and miracles.

Meg Cabot

Proposal

Uno

IT WAS VALENTINE'S DAY, and where was I?

Freezing my butt off in a cemetery, that's where. Romantic, right?

But I had a job to do, and that job required that I sit in the dark on a headstone, and wait for a ghost to show up.

Yeah. That's the kind of girl I am, unfortunately. Not the candy-and-stuffed-bear kind. The I-see-dead-people kind.

Discomfort from the cold aside, I was actually kind of okay with the situation. Would I have preferred to be at one of those cute little outdoor bistros over on Ocean Ave, snuggling under a heat lamp and sipping champagne while dining on the Valentine's Day surf and turf special with my one true love?

Of course.

I wouldn't even have minded being back at the dorm, hanging out at my suite mates' anti–Valentine's Day party, swigging cheap vodka and cranberry juice cocktails while making sarcastic comments about the romcoms we all claimed to hate (but secretly loved, of course).

But me and my one true love? We'd agreed to spend this Valentine's Day apart.

Hey, it's all right. We're mature adults. We don't need a stupid holiday named after some martyred saint to tell us when to say I love you.

And okay, the last place anyone wants to be on Valentine's Day is a cemetery. Anyone except spooks, I mean, and those of us who were born with the curse (or gift, depending on how you choose to look at it) of communicating with them.

But I didn't mind. Monterey's Cementerio El Encinal was kind of soothing. It was just me, the headstones, and the marine layer rolling in from the Pacific, making it a bit chillier than it had been when I'd gotten there half an hour ago, and a bit more difficult to see the grave I had staked out.

But who cared if my blow-out was turning limp from the humidity, or my nose red from the chill? It wasn't like I had a date.

Well, with anyone who personally mattered to me.

And I knew this guy was going to show up sooner or later, since he'd done so every night this past week, like clockwork, to the bewilderment—and fear—of the community.

At least when I got home, I'd have a nice cocktail waiting for me.

This guy I was expecting? He had nothing waiting for him—nothing good, anyway.

I just hoped he'd show up before my butt cheeks froze to the headstone I was sitting on. I wished Mrs. J. Charles Peterson III had chosen a softer material than granite to mark her husband's final resting place. Marble, perhaps. Or cashmere. Cashmere would have been a nice choice, though it probably wouldn't have lasted long given the harsh elements of the Northern California coast.

When you've been in the ghost-busting business as long as I have (twenty-one years), you learn a few things. The first one is, spectral stakeouts are boring.

The second one is, there isn't anything you can do to entertain yourself during them, because the minute you slip in earbuds to listen to music or watch a video on your iPod or start texting with your boyfriend on your phone (assuming he'll text back, which, considering mine was born around the time Queen Victoria inherited the throne and thinks modern technology is dehumanizing), whoever—or whatever—it is you're waiting for is going to show up, hit you over the head, and run off while you were distracted.

Three, if you bring along a thermos containing a delicious warm beverage—coffee or hot chocolate or hot cider spiked with Bacardi—you will have to pee in about fifteen minutes, and the moment you pull down your jeans to do so (apologies, J. Charles), you will, literally, be caught with your pants down.

These are the things they never portray in the dozens of movies and television shows there've been over the years about people with my ability. Mediating between the living and the dead is a thankless job, but someone's got to do it.

I was sitting there wondering why Mrs. J. Charles Peterson III hadn't installed an eternal flame at her husband's grave so I could warm my hands (and butt) when I finally saw him—or it—moving through the mist like a wraith.

But he was no wraith. He was your average, ordinary dirtbag NCDP—or Non-Compliant Deceased Person, as those in my trade refer to those who refuse to cross over to the other side.

He headed directly for the grave across from J. Charles Peterson's. He was so fixated by it, he didn't so much as glance in my direction.

I couldn't really blame him. The recently deceased have reason to be preoccupied. They have the whole I-just-died thing going on.

But this guy had more than the fact that he'd recently died on his mind. I knew, because his post-mortem activities had been causing me—and the entire Monterey Bay area—aggravation for days. Even the local news—and several popular media blogs—had commented on it.

Which was why, of course, I was spending my Valentine's Day sitting on a headstone waiting for him, instead of hanging with my homegirls back at the dorm, drinking Cape Codders and tearing Katherine Heigl a new one.

I watched as the guy—only a few years younger than me, but dressed about the same, in a black tee, leather jacket, and black jeans and boots, as well—bent and removed the fresh flowers that had been lovingly placed on the grave in front of him. Today's batch were red, and, in honor of the holiday, arranged in a heart shape.

True, as floral arrangements went, they weren't to my taste. I'd have gone for something more classic—a dozen long-stemmed roses, perhaps. Definitely nothing Valentine's themed. That seemed a little gauche to me.

Of course, I hope not to be dead for a long, long time, and when I am, I doubt I'll care what anyone puts on my grave. Also, I want to be cremated, so it won't be an issue.

But I still wouldn't have done what that no-good NCDP did, which was rude, regardless of how objectionable he found the floral design:

He lifted the heart arrangement off the grave, tossed it in the air, then drop-kicked it, causing it to explode into a gentle hailstorm of petals.

"Nice," I said. "Very nice, mature behavior. I'm sure your mother would be proud."

The NCDP whirled around, startled.

"What the hell!" His eyes were as round as if he, not me, were the one seeing a ghost. "What are you—how can you—*who are you*?"

"I'm Suze Simon," I said. "And you thought being dead was bad? Buddy, your eternal nightmare's only just begun."

Dos

Everybody's got a secret.

Maybe you've told a lie. Maybe you cheated on a test. Maybe—like the Non-Compliant Deceased Person standing in front of me—you've killed someone (I really hope not, for your sake).

The thing about secrets, though, is that they get out. And trust me, if you've got a secret, eventually, it's *going* to get out.

And when it does, things are probably going to turn out to be okay . . . well, after some counseling, or at worst, some jail time, or—if you're a celebrity—maybe a tell-all book with a couple of talk show appearances thrown in, to apologize to your disappointed fans.

Not this guy's secret, though.

And not mine, either. All the counseling, jail time, and TV talk shows in the world are never going to make *my* secret okay. My secret is the kind that religious leaders in every culture in every society in the world have railed against at one time or another, claiming that it's an abomination, unnatural, the work of the devil. Throughout history, women with my secret have been burned at the stake, drowned, or pelted with stones until they were dead. The scientific community has declared my secret "incompatible with the well-established laws of science," and therefore nonexistent.

Which is why, of course, writers (and producers, and movie and television audiences) *love* my secret. In the past decade alone there've been scores of books, television dramas, movies, video games, and even reality shows based on people who have my secret ability. Most of them have scored pretty decent ratings, too.

None of them have gotten it right, though. A few have come close. Startlingly close.

Close enough that lately I've had to work harder than ever to appear like the cool, collected, fashion-forward twenty-something girl I seem to be . . . on the *outside*, anyway.

Only a couple of people have figured out what a weirdo super freak I am on the *inside*. And those people all have reason to keep my secret, because . . . well, I've helped them resolve their own secrets.

One person especially. Miraculously, he fell in love with me.

Don't ask me why. *I* think I'm fabulous, but I'm not entirely sure what he sees in me (except the fact that I've saved his life a few times. But he's returned the favor).

The only reason we aren't spending this February

fourteenth together is because he's currently enrolled in medical school four hours away, and he's doing rotations (and also still interviewing for residencies).

Yeah, my boyfriend's in *medical school*. He wants to be a pediatrician. He's hoping to get a residency at St. Francis Hospital nearby (the medical school residency "matching program" is this whole big thing. He finds out where—and *if*—he's been matched next month), but I'm not optimistic. We've already been so lucky simply *finding* one another, it seems selfish to wish for more.

What a guy like him is even doing with a girl like me, I still can't figure out . . . but then again, Hector "Jesse" de Silva has secrets, too. And some of them are even darker than mine.

Not darker than the guy's with whom I was spending my Valentine's Day, though, that's for sure.

"Let's just say I'm your fairy godmother," I said to him, lowering myself from J. Charles Peterson's grave. I'd like to say I did it gracefully, but I'm afraid I did not, due to butt freeze. I tried not to let it show, however. "And I'm here to make you sure you get to the ball on time. Only in this case, the ball is the afterlife. Come on, if we hurry, you can still make it before midnight. Only I'm not sure Cinderella"—I pointed at the grave the NCDP had just desecrated—"will be there waiting for you. Or that if she is, she'll be too happy to see you."

The NCDP still seemed startled. He wasn't exactly my idea of Prince Charming, but his girlfriend—a pretty, popular, honor student—had evidently found something in him to love.

"Y-you can see me?" he stammered, his eyes narrowing behind his black-framed glasses. He had the whole look down—whatever look it was that he was going for, some kind of tortured artist/Steve Jobs thing, except that this kid was black. I dress in dark colors for night jobs so as not to be noticeable to security guards. He seemed to be wearing it to express the darkness of his soul. "No one—no one has been able to see me since the accident."

Accident. That was a nice touch.

"Obviously I can see you, genius," I said. "And I'm not the only one." I jerked a thumb over my shoulder at the towering oak tree just beyond J. Charles Peterson's grave. Cementerio El Encinal meant *Cemetery of Many Oaks* (I'm taking Spanish so that when Jesse and I have kids, I'll understand what he's saying when he yells at them in his mother tongue). "Your girlfriend's family got tired of finding all of their floral arrangements kicked to bits, so they installed a security camera three days ago. Your little antics have gone viral. They even made the nightly news."

He stared in the direction of the video camera. "Really?" But instead of looking ashamed of his disrespectful behavior toward his beloved's grave, his face broke out into a grin. "Cool."

The contempt I'd been feeling for him kicked up a couple of notches, which is never a good thing in a mediation. We're supposed to feel nothing toward our "clients"—nothing except compassion.

But it's hard to feel compassion toward a cold-blooded murderer.

"Uh, no, not cool," I snarled. "And don't go waving to

Mom just yet. For one thing, I disabled the camera for the night. And for another, you're dead, in case it still hasn't sunk in. You have no physical presence anymore—at least to anyone but people like myself. All that camera records when you show up is static. People think it's a—"

"Ghost?" He smirked.

God, this kid was a pill.

"Some of the less reputable news outlets speculate it might be a ghost," I admitted. "Others think it's a pair of vandals working in tandem, one destroying the flowers while the other messes with the camera. Others think the family is trying to perpetrate a hoax on the media and law enforcement, who take grave desecration seriously. That's not a very nice thing to do to people who are going through a period of mourning over the death of a beloved daughter."

That, at least, sunk in. He stopped smirking and scowled at the grave he'd just vandalized. It had a brand-new headstone over it, in pink marble, the kind with a photo etched beside the name.

Jasmin Ahmadi, the epitaph read. *Beloved daughter, sister, friend. Too soon taken, forever to be missed.*

The photo showed a dark-haired girl laughing into the camera, a twinkle in her eyes. Jasmin had been seventeen years old at her time of death.

His headstone was a few rows over, but it was much simpler, flat gray granite with an epitaph listing only his name—Mark Rodgers—and dates of birth and death. There was no photo. The year of his birth—and date of his death—was the same as Jasmin's.

"Ultimately it doesn't matter what people think," I said. "Ghost, vandals, whatever. Because it's going to stop tonight, Mark."

Instead of apologizing—or offering an explanation—for his behavior, Mark only looked more disgruntled. "If they don't want me taking the flowers off her grave, they should stop leaving them. Especially *him*."

This was not the response I was expecting. "Him? Him who?"

"*Him*. Zack." Mark's mouth twisted as if the name was distasteful.

I had no idea what he was talking about.

"Look, Mark," I said. "I hate to be the one to break it to you, but people are going to leave flowers on your girlfriend's grave. She was very popular and died tragically at a young age."

"*I* died at a young age," Mark snapped, jabbing a thumb at his own chest. "And you'll notice no one is leaving flowers on *my* grave!"

He pointed accusingly in the direction of his final resting place. I couldn't see it, given the darkness and the fog, but I'd taken a look before assuming my post on J. Charles Peterson's headstone, so I knew he was right. No one had left so much as a pebble on his grave to indicate that they'd visited there since he'd been buried.

"Yeah," I said. "Well, maybe that's something you should have thought about before you killed your girlfriend, and then yourself, because she said no when you proposed."

Tres

MARK SHOOK OFF the hand I'd placed on his shoulder, his gaze wild.

"What?" he cried, appalled. "No! *That's* what people think, that I killed her? But that isn't what happened *at all*. I would never hurt Jasmin!"

"Sure," I said, in my most soothing tone.

As a psych major—did I mention that I'm in school, too? Not medical school, like Jesse. I'm still only an undergrad.

But I'm majoring in psychology. And after graduation, I'm going for a master's in counseling. I want to help kids like I was, kids who have secrets they feel like they can't tell anyone. Since I was one of those kids, I'll know how to recognize them, and hopefully be able to help them.

Well, except the ones I'm too late to help, like Jasmin. And Mark.

"Look," I said to him, as he continued to stare at me

in disbelief. Sometimes it takes a while for it to sink in to spirits, especially young ones, that they're dead, and how they died—even when they're the ones responsible for said death. "What's done is done. You can't go back and change it. You can only move forward. Jasmin has, which is why she isn't here. And now it's time for you to move forward, too, Mark."

"M-move forward?" He looked confused.

"Yes. To your next life, the afterlife, heaven, hell, whatever." I didn't want to get too technical about it because I don't really know where spirits go after I encourage them to step into the light. All I have to do is get them there. "You can't hang around here, though, taking out your anger issues on Jasmin's grave. That isn't healthy for anyone, especially you."

"I'm not talking about *anyone*. I'm talking about that asshole Zack Farhat. He keeps coming and putting flowers on Jasmin's grave, which isn't right, because—"

"Sure," I said, still using my fake soothing tone. "The thing is, Mark, the sooner you start letting things like this Zack guy go, the sooner you can be with her."

I was completely lying. I didn't think for one minute that Mark was going to get to be with Jasmin in his next life—or wherever he was going—after what he'd done to her. But lying to him seemed like the quickest way to get the job over with. "It doesn't matter anymore."

"Yes, it does," he said. "It *does* matter. Why do you keep saying it doesn't matter? And why do you keep saying *I* killed Jasmin. I didn't."

The temperature had begun to drop—which was

odd, since I'd checked the weather on my phone before coming out, and it had said we were in for a warm front. This should have been my first clue, but I missed it. Of course I missed it. I was so angry over what he'd done, I'd let my emotions cloud my common sense.

"I'm saying those things don't matter, Mark. They don't because you and Jasmin are dead. You both died instantly when you slammed your car into the side of that cliff out by Rocky Creek Bridge last week. Remember? You should. You were the one who was driving."

It was at that exact moment that the wind picked up, and the fog began to swirl around us, along with some of the stray petals from the floral arrangement Mark had destroyed.

But even then, I didn't realize what was going on.

"That isn't how it happened *at all*!" Mark thundered. "I would *never* do that! I would never hurt Jasmin. I told you, *I loved her*!"

"Yeah, we all know how much you loved her, Mark." I can't believe I didn't pick up on the signals then. But he'd really pissed me off. Murderers have a tendency to do that. "I know you proposed in the restaurant—all the servers saw you get down on one knee and present her with your grandmother's ring. They said it was incredibly sweet. But in the car, something happened, didn't it? It must have, because no one could find the ring in the wreckage. It wasn't on Jasmin's finger, and it wasn't in its velvet box anymore, either. What happened to it, Mark? Did you two have a fight coming home? Did she change her mind, and toss it out the window? Is that why you slammed your car into that cliff?"

His face had gone bloodless—as bloodless as it was possible for a ghost to look. That was all the encouragement I needed to go on, even though it was the worst thing I could have done.

But it was cold, and it was Valentine's Day, and I was in a cemetery with a boy who'd selfishly killed his girlfriend and now wouldn't even allow others to leave flowers on her grave.

"Yeah," I plunged on recklessly. "That's what I thought. They'll never find that ring, because that's a coastal road, and it's probably at the bottom of the ocean by now. But that's why you killed her, isn't it? Because she rejected you. You're both so young, and she was going away to an Ivy League college next year, while you're grades weren't so good, so you were staying here and going to community college because that's the only place you got in— which there's no shame in, believe me. I go to one, too. But maybe proposing to her was your way of trying to force her to be faithful to you while she was away, and in the heat of the moment, she accepted. But then the closer the two of you got to home, the more she realized what a mistake she'd made, so she—"

"*No!*" he roared, so loudly that I was surprised people from homes and businesses nearby didn't come running outside to see what was going on.

But there's only one other person besides me in the Monterey Bay area who could pick up on spectral sound waves—especially now that Jesse is going to school so far away—and that person happened to be away at a seminarian retreat in New Mexico. I knew because Father Dominic likes to keep his present (and former) students up to date on his daily activities on Facebook.

The day my old high school principal started his own Facebook account was the day I swore off social media forever. So far this has worked out fine since I prefer face-to-face interactions. It's easier to tell when people are lying.

Unless, of course, they're ghosts. Then it gets a little tougher.

Now the wind was really picking up. Not only that, but the temperature had plunged another four or five degrees, seemingly in the past few seconds, which was, of course, impossible.

But so is what I do for a living. Which I'd really like to give up, because in addition to being dangerous, I don't even get paid. At least as a guidance counselor, I'll have a salary, 401K, and health benefits.

"Look, Mark," I said, ducking as a memorial stake vase that had been uprooted by the strong wind sailed in my direction, then clanged against J. Charles Peterson's headstone. "Road rage is incredibly common. Almost seven million car accidents occur a year because of it. I get that maybe you didn't *mean* to do it. But if Jasmin didn't throw that ring out, where did it go? Until you admit it, you're going to be stuck here on this plane of existence, which isn't going to do you any good—"

"I'm telling you, I didn't do it!" Mark roared. "And she

didn't throw away the ring! It was Zack. It has to be. *He* did it!"

Floral arrangements from other graves began to whiz by, traveling dangerously close to my head. I was being pelted with flowers, which sounds pleasant, but isn't. Those things hurt when being whipped at high velocity by the wind.

"I thought I saw his pickup in the parking lot at the restaurant, but Jasmin said I was being paranoid," Mark went on. "Then I saw the headlights behind us out on the coastal road."

"Wait . . ." I said, from behind the arms I'd flung up to protect my face from the dead bouquets being hurled in my direction. "What?"

But it was too late. Far, far too late. Too late for Mark and Jasmin, too late for Zack, and maybe too late for me, too.

"Why won't anyone listen to me?" Mark demanded. "He had his brights on, but I still recognized that stupid souped-up monster truck of his. He was going way over the speed limit, which was forcing me to go over the speed limit, too. And you know there's that lane closure just past Rocky Creek Bridge—"

I felt my stomach lurch. I had seen this on the news.

I had seen a lot on the news.

The problem was, I'd listened to it. I'd believed it. Me, the girl whose kind the media insist don't exist. Why would I believe *anything* they said?

"Mark," I said. Clouds scudded across what had earlier been a clear night sky, which was odd, because the weather app on my phone hadn't said a word about rain. Thunder rumbled, and suddenly, in addition to flowers, I was being pelted with hard, stinging rain. "Are you sure—?"

"What do you mean, am I sure?" he snapped. "Yeah, I'm sure. I'm telling you, it was him. I don't remember what happened after that, but ever since I woke up, I've been watching him put flowers on *my* girl's grave."

This was not good. This was not good at all. "Mark—"

"And now you're telling me everyone thinks *I* killed her, and that he's some kind of saint, and I need to move on?"

I swallowed, using my arms to shield my head from the pouring rain. "Okay, look," I said. "I wasn't aware of *all* of the facts in the case until recently, Mark. But now that I am, why don't we take some time to re-evaluate the situation and—"

"Take some time to re-evaluate the situation?" Mark echoed. He was in tears, and I didn't blame him. I felt like crying myself. "No thanks. Now that you told me what's really going on, I think I have a better proposal. And it sure as hell isn't that I should move on, or take some time to re-evaluate the situation."

"Mark," I yelled. I had to yell in order to be heard over the thunder and rain. "Don't. Seriously. Don't do anything you might regret. If what you're telling me is true, then you have a really good chance right now of joining Jasmin, wherever she is. But if you do what I think you're about to do, you're going to lose that chance forever. Come with me instead. I'll help you cross over, and then

I'll take care of this Zack person. That's my job, not yours. You really don't want to—"

But it was too late. In a swirl of tears and rain and rose petals, he was gone.

And I was screwed.

Cuatro

WHEN I GOT back to my dorm that night, it was bedlam, and not just because of the sudden "super cell" that had swept into the tri-county area, soaking me to the bone and causing flash flooding on roads throughout Monterey Bay.

It was also because there was a man in my room.

Did I mention that I live in an all-girl dorm? Probably not, because it's too embarrassing. It wasn't my idea, believe me. It was my stepdad's.

I guess I lucked out in some ways despite my alleged "gift," since even though my birth dad died when I was little, the guy my mom married back when I was in high school (and for whom she moved across the country, dragging me from Brooklyn, NY, to Carmel, CA, when I was sixteen), turned out to be pretty decent.

Upside: Andy adores my mom, has his own home improvement show (which recently went into syndication, so he and my mom are currently swimming in payola), and is an amazing cook.

Downside: He has three sons—none of whom I have ever even remotely considered boning, sexy-erotic-novel style—and, being almost as Catholic as my boyfriend, is way, way too overprotective.

So I guess shouldn't have been surprised when I was applying for campus housing and overheard Andy telling my mother that the only way I was going to be safe from all the sexual assaults he'd heard about on National Public Radio was if I lived in an all-girl dorm.

Never mind that I have been kicking the butts of the undead since I was in elementary school, and that almost the entire time I resided under Andy's roof, I had a hot undead guy living in my bedroom. These are two of those secrets I was telling you about. Andy doesn't know about them, and neither does my mother. They think Jesse is what Father Dominic told them he is: a "young Jesuit student who transferred to the Carmel Mission from Mexico, then lost his yearning to go into the priesthood" after meeting me.

That one slays me every time.

So I didn't protest the decision. I didn't do so well on the SATs (the things people like me are good at, you can't measure with a multiple-choice test, let alone an essay), much to the everlasting mortification of my high-achieving, feminist mother. It didn't help that my best friends CeeCee, Adam, and Gina got into extremely good schools, boosting my mom's dream that I was going to Harvard and live in Kirkland House, like Facebook founder Mark Zuckerberg.

Instead the only place I got into was the local community college, where I live in a suite in what's not-so-jokingly referred to as the Virgin Vault, with a practicing witch, a klepto, and a girl whose family's religion doesn't allow her speak to men outside of their faith.

I keep assuring Mom it's cool. Another one of our suite mates came out last semester as a lesbian (to the surprise of none of us but herself), and a fifth is sleeping with a guy who's in an actual motorcycle gang.

"See, Mom?" I'd told her. "Way better than Harvard. There's so much more diversity!"

Like most of my jokes, she didn't find that one funny.

But, seriously, these are my girls, each and every one of them. I'm secretly doing case studies on each of them for my biological psych class.

Except that tonight I didn't have time to stop and chat, let alone have a friendly cocktail. I needed to change out of my sopping wet clothes, find out where this Zack guy lived, and then get back out there and stop Mark Rodgers from making the biggest mistake of his life.

Well, of his death, if you wanted to get technical about it.

But the girls were all in an uproar, as I discovered as soon as I keyed in with my ID card.

"What the hell is going on?" I asked Lauren, the witch. The rest of the girls from our floor were in the common room on beanbag chairs in front of the television, on which a film starring Drew Barrymore was playing (we each have single bedrooms while sharing a communal bathroom, kitchen, and TV slash study slash common area, *Orange Is the New Black* prison style, though to date no one has been shanked).

The game was that every time Drew or one of her zany coworkers wondered whether or not men were worth it, we were all supposed to chug.

But the game got suspended when I walked in. Everyone turned, raised their red cups, and started squealing.

"There's a surprise for you in your room," Lauren said, handing me a cocktail. "Where were you, anyway? I tried to call to tell you, but it went straight to voice mail. I was worried you'd been caught in that storm. And"—she nodded at my dripping hair—"I see that you were."

"Library," I said, taking a single grateful gulp of the cocktail. I couldn't let myself have more, since I was going to be driving again in a few minutes, to wherever Zack Farhat lived. "Studying."

"Ha," she said, with a grin. "You, studying, at the library. Good one!"

"Ha." I smiled back at her. "Yeah, I know. I was at the mall."

"Sure you were. Here." She plucked something off her desk. "This came for you. It was too big to fit in your mailbox, so they left it on the shelf for you to pick up downstairs, but I was afraid Ashley might swipe it, so I grabbed it." Ashley was our resident klepto. She was making progress with her therapist, but like anyone with an impulse control disorder, she had to take it one day at a time. "Looks like someone's got a Valentine."

I glanced down at the package, excited that it might be

from Jesse, even though we'd agreed we weren't going to contribute to the mass hysteria surrounding Valentine's Day, since we loved each other unconditionally every day, and he didn't think I was the sort of girl who needed reminding of that fact with a cheap mass-produced card, candy, or stuffed bear.

(Not to mention that Valentine's Day was no longer the sweet tradition it was when he was a child, when people used the Pony Express to send handmade greetings to their sweethearts. See what I mean about some of his secrets being a little on the dark side?)

He was partly right. I don't care about cards, and I haven't owned a stuffed animal since I saw my first supernatural entity when I was a toddler.

Candy I wouldn't have minded, though. What girl doesn't like candy?

Nor would I have said no to a dinner at one of those bistros I'd passed on my drive out to the cemetery. Those couples snuggled under those heat lamps looked so happy and contented, I wanted to pull over and snuggle up next to them.

Snuggle up next to them or pound their faces in out of jealousy. I wasn't sure which.

But I'd never have mentioned a word of this to Jesse, because I didn't want him to think I was the kind of girl who'd enjoy being taken out for what was undoubtedly grossly overpriced, probably not even very good surf and turf on a night that—he was right—has turned into a completely manufactured, mass-produced, grotesque commercial modern holiday.

Plus I didn't want to stress him out while he was interviewing for residencies.

Besides, our time was going to come . . . after we'd both graduated from our separate schools and were helping others to overcome their own deep dark secrets the way we have.

Note sarcasm. Not that I doubted Jesse was going to be hugely successful at his chosen profession. I just wasn't sure about the overcoming-our-dark-secrets part. It might take a while for Jesse to move past having been murdered and then forced to live as a paranormal being for a century and a half.

And given the mess I'd made of tonight's mediation, I'd say my chance at being even a passable school counselor was nil, at best.

So I wasn't that surprised when I glanced in the upper left-hand corner of the obscenely large red envelope Lauren had handed me and saw that it wasn't from Jesse. It was from someone I recognized, however. Only too well.

Paul Slater.

My own Zack Farhat.

I felt a chill up my spine that had nothing to do with my wet hair and sopping clothing.

"Thanks, Lauren," I said, and hastily shoved the envelope into my messenger bag. "I'll just go change and then join you guys for a quick drink. Then I have to dash out again. I, uh, have an errand to run."

"Or maybe not," screamed several of the more sociable girls from in front of the TV.

But since they were always saying stuff like this, I didn't think much of it . . .

Until I threw open the door to my room and found six feet or so of unadulterated Spanish-American male hotness stretched out on my bed.

"Oh," Jesse said, lowering the review book he was reading for Step 2 of his USMLE exams. "You're home. Finally. I was getting worried."

"Oh, boy." I was too shocked to think of anything more witty to say. "Am I glad to see *you*."

I leaped on him like a long lost dog on its owner. I did everything but lick his face. I probably licked his face a little, actually. It was embarrassing, but it's a very nice face.

"Well," he said, when I finally let him up for air. "If I'd known this was how you were going to say hello, I'd have gotten here sooner."

"What are you doing here?" I asked a little breathlessly. There were parts of him I could feel pressing against me that I definitely wanted to feel more closely, but both of us were fully clothed, making the kind of closeness I was hoping for impossible without some disassembly. "I thought you had rotations or interviews or a lobotomy to perform or something."

"So you do pay attention when I tell you what I do on a daily basis," he said drily. "How sweet. Actually, I wanted to surprise you. I've been waiting here for you for hours." He held up his cell phone. "Do you ever actually check your messages?"

"Sorry, my phone was off. Then it got soaked, and wouldn't turn on. I was—"

"Don't even try to tell me you were at the library." Amusement danced in his night dark eyes. "You might have fooled your friends with that one, *querida*, but you'll never fool me. Where were you, really? And could you put down that drink? I think you've christened us both enough for now."

"Oh, sorry." I set my V and C on the floor, then peeled off my messenger bag and coat, and dropped them beside it. I didn't want to kill the mood by telling him the truth about how I'd been off nearly being murdered by an NCDP. He had a tendency to get cranky when he heard that kind of thing. He was even more overprotective than my stepfather. But in a boyfriend, that kind of thing is actually attractive. "I was helping out a friend who's flunking Statistics. But you know what? That's boring, let's get back to you. What are you doing here, for real? I thought we agreed that Valentine's Day has become a gross commercial holiday and we don't believe in it."

"We don't," he said. I didn't miss the appreciative way his dark-eyed gaze flicked over my form-fitting tee, which had gotten damp despite my leather jacket. Yeah, I've still got it. "But this morning a few people at the hospital were discussing what they were doing tonight for Valentine's Day with their significant others, and when I mentioned that we don't believe in the holiday, they—"

"Properly shamed you?" I threw myself on top of him again. "Oh, my God, give me their addresses so I can send them all fruit baskets."

He held me close. The bulge was still there. I could feel

it, hard as a rock, against my stomach. I snuggled my face to his neck, inhaling. I didn't think I'll ever get enough of the smell of him, though it's changed over the years, from a combination of smoke and old, leather-bound books to the clean, sharp odor of antiseptic soap, thanks to the many times a day he has to wash his hands due to the patients he sees on rotations.

I never knew the smell of antiseptic soap could be so sexy.

"Some of the doctors said I might need to reorganize my priorities, yes." He grinned up at me. "So I did. I got in the car and started driving."

"But how did you get in *here*?" I asked, pretending I had no idea what was going on below his waist. "Men aren't allowed in the Virgin Vault."

"Apparently exceptions can be made for dashing young med students who come bearing restaurant reservations." He glanced at his watch. "Which we've now missed."

"Oh, Jesse, I'm sorry. If you'd called me sooner I could have changed my schedule." Which would have been immensely preferable to the mess I'd created in the cemetery. "Where were we going to go?"

"It was too late to get a reservation anywhere decent," he said. "And besides, I couldn't afford it on my impoverished student budget. So I was going to take you on a picnic at the beach, to watch the sunset."

I felt even worse. "Oh, my God. Were we going to snuggle under a blanket next to a bonfire?"

"Yes. Although considering this storm, which seems

to have come out of nowhere, I suppose it's just as well my plans fell through."

I refrained from mentioning that I'd caused the storm, the torrential rain from which I could still hear pelting my window. Well, not me, but my client, who'd gone from being merely non-compliant to murderous.

Was it wrong of me suddenly not to care? From what Mark had said, it sounded like Zack Farhat deserved what he had coming.

Okay, yeah, this was wrong of me.

"It was going to be very romantic," Jesse was saying. "I even brought champagne. Well, not real champagne, since I can't afford that. It's sparkling wine, from California—"

"I prefer sparkling wine from California," I interrupted. "California is the state of your birth."

"But now," he went on, lifting a bottle from the far side of my bed, "it's warm. It wouldn't fit in your miniature refrigerator. You have too many energy drinks in there. Susannah, you should stay away from those things. You know they're full of—"

"Minifridge," I corrected him. "It's called a mini-fridge, not a miniature refrigerator. And I like warm champagne."

"No one likes warm champagne, Susannah, even when it's from the state of my birth. Now, why don't you change out of those wet things, and—"

"Climb into bed with you?" I asked. "That sounds like a really, really good idea."

"—and stop lying to me about where you were tonight."

Cinco

I FROZE, MY shirt halfway over my head.

"Wait. How could you tell I was lying?"

"You can't even balance your checkbook. Who would ask for your help with Statistics?"

I tossed my shirt to the floor. It was slightly disconcerting that he hadn't even noticed I was wearing only a bra (and jeans), but that's one of the downsides of dating someone who'd lived with you for years, even if he'd been in spirit form at the time and chivalrously only materialized when you were fully clothed. I'd always imagined he'd been too irritatingly faithful to his Roman Catholic upbringing—and his Victorian-era roots—ever to have considered spying on me, but now I wasn't too sure.

Except of course that since I'd managed to reunite his soul with his body a few years ago—another skill of mine that, sadly, cannot be measured by the SATs—he refused to go further than second base (third on the rare occasions he drank more than three glasses of wine) with me out of "respect" for what he thinks he owes to me—and my family and Father Dominic and the church—for all we've done for him, giving him a second chance at life, blah blah blah blah.

Sometimes I get so sick of hearing about it. All I want to do is *bone*, like a normal couple.

But we can't, because we aren't normal (although normal isn't considered a therapeutically beneficial term), and my boyfriend has post-traumatic stress from being dead. And is also Catholic and a century and a half years old, of course, even though he doesn't look a day over twenty-six.

"I happen to be making a B in Statistics, Jesse," I said. "That's above average. And no one balances their check-book. No one even *has* a checkbook anymore, except for you and Father Dominic."

"Stop avoiding the subject, *querida*." He regarded me impassively from the bed. "And stop thinking you'll distract me from it, too, by undressing in front of me."

Damn.

"Fine." I snatched a dry shirt from my school-issued dresser. "If you must know, I was at the cemetery."

He raised one dark eyebrow—the one with the scar through it, a perfect crescent moon of brown skin where dark hair should have been. "Cemetery?" he echoed.

Then indignation swiftly replaced bewilderment.

"Was *that* what I felt earlier?" he demanded, rising from the bed. "I thought it was because you were out there driving in this storm. But that wasn't it, was it? It was because you were chasing a ghost, alone, in a cemetery, *at night*."

I'd begun peeling off my boots. I know he'd asked me not to undress in front of him, but my jeans were soaked. I needed to change them.

Okay, they might have not been *that* wet. But I needed time to come up with a reply that wouldn't enrage him. This was an evasive maneuver.

"Jesse, I don't know what you're talking about. What do you mean, what you felt earlier?"

"You know exactly what I'm talking about. We may no longer have a ghost-mediator connection, Susannah, but I can still tell when you're feeling afraid, and earlier this evening, you were very, very afraid—"

Now I was the one who felt indignant. I nearly dropped one of my boots.

"Afraid? I wasn't afraid of that little brat. I just didn't enjoy being pelted by funerary floral arrangements, that's all."

"Susannah." Now he was looming over me, seventy-three inches or so of tasty man-meat. "*What happened in the cemetery?*"

Susannah.

I felt another chill down my spine, but unlike the one I'd felt when I'd seen the name *Paul Slater* on the envelope Lauren had handed me, this one was pleasant.

As hard as it is to date someone with nineteenth-century manners—seriously, it's getting to a point where I spend so much time swimming laps in the campus pool to work off my sexual frustration, my highlights are becoming brassy—I still feel a thrill every time Jesse calls me Susannah. He thinks the name everyone else calls me—Suze—is too short and ugly for someone of my strength and beauty.

Yeah. He gets me. Well, except for the part where I'm totally fine with premarital sex and am also convinced that God, if he or she exists, is, too.

"Well," I said, since he was still looming over me, looking more like a dominating he-male than a nerdy doctor-to-be. I had no choice but to tell him, even though I knew it was going to make him mad. "Okay, so there's this NCDP who's been stealing flowers off his dead girlfriend's grave, and the girl's family got it on video—well, static is what they mostly got, but it's been freaking everybody out—I'm surprised you haven't seen it, it's been all over the news. But I guess you've been busy with your studying and interviews and stuff. So, anyway, I decided to go check it out tonight." I wiggled out of my jeans. "And long story short, this guy, Mark, says—"

"*Susannah.*" My name came out in a frustrated hiss. When I glanced in his direction, I saw that Jesse had turned to face my window, the curtains of which he'd closed, so no one could see that a resident of the Virgin Vault was entertaining a contraband man in her room.

He had his arms folded across his chest and his dark head bent, his gaze fastened to the floor. I felt a surge of shame for my bad behavior—but not for my black hipster briefs, which even I have to admit I look pretty hot in.

"Sorry," I said, pulling open a drawer and grabbing a dry pair of jeans. "But you're the one who told me to change out of my wet things."

"Not in front of me," he ground out. "I'm not a eunuch."

"Oh, believe me, I *know*. But you're the one who says we have to wait until we get married to have sex, and that we can't get married until you can financially support us both, which is just about the most ridiculously chauvinistic thing I ever—"

"Can we not have this conversation again *right now*?" he questioned over his shoulder. "I've told you, I respect you and your family both too much to be a financial burden—"

"I thought you said you didn't want to have this conversation again right now."

"Are you finished dressing?"

I zipped up my fly. "Yes."

He turned around. His angular jaw—beneath a dusting of five o'clock shadow—had a slight flush to it, and his dark eyes were brighter than ever. "What happened in the cemetery? Did he hurt you?"

"Geez, of course not." I thought it better not to mention the vases, or that Mark seemed to have been the one who'd whipped up the super cell. That was probably only a coincidence, anyway.

Except that in my business, there are no coincidences. Had it been a coincidence that of all the houses in all the world, I'd just happened to move into the one Jesse had been murdered in?

I think not.

But if there is some higher power in charge of all this stuff, he or she has some explaining to do. Because why would they put someone like me in charge of mediating a case like Mark's? I was already doing a supremely crappy job of it, if the expression on Jesse's face as I described to him what had happened in the cemetery—well, an abridged version, anyway—was any indication. How I'd gone there to convince Mark to move on, and how he'd revealed to me that he couldn't, because he hadn't actually killed Jasmin (like everyone thought), and how he was now convinced he had to go get revenge on the person who (allegedly) had.

"But technically it isn't my fault," I said in my own defense. "How was I supposed to know there'd been a second vehicle involved in the accident? Nothing in any of the news reports mentioned that. You would think there'd have been skid marks or broken glass or paint from the other car or something— "

He had me in his arms so fast, I hardly knew what was happening. One second he'd been over by the window, and the next, he was crushing me in his embrace. He may not have been a ghost anymore, but he could certainly move as rapidly as one when he felt like it.

"Thank God you weren't hurt," he said, burying his face in my rain-dampened hair. "Susannah, how could you have been so foolish as to have gone there alone?"

"Well," I said. The hug was surprising, but not unwelcome, especially since I enjoyed the feel of his rockhard chest against me, and in particular the familiar tingle from the general vicinity of my pubic bone I always experienced whenever it came into contact with any part of his anatomy. "I didn't have a choice. Father

Dominic is away at some ministry conference. And I didn't know you were coming. If you'd called sooner, I'd have waited for—"

"You can't go on doing this, *querida*," he said, shoving me roughly away from him so he could look down into my eyes. But he still held on to my shoulders, so I couldn't get away. Not that I wanted to. "I've already lost everyone I've ever loved. I can't lose you, too."

"Jesse, you're not going to lose me. I had the situation totally under control." Sort of. "But I have to say that after so many years of you keeping your feelings for me hidden out of propriety, it's really nice to hear you say all those things. Plus, it's emotionally healthy that you're letting them out in this way. Keep unburdening yourself." I wrapped my arms around his neck. "What is it exactly, that you find so irresistible about me? Is it my magnetic personality? Or my emerald green eyes? Or maybe it's just my hot bod?" I felt something against my torso. "Oh, I'm getting the impression that it's my hot bod."

He thrust me away from him again, this time looking insulted. "This is nothing to joke about, Susannah. If that boy had murder on his mind when you left him, he may not stop at killing only his rival for his sweetheart's affections. *You* may also be on his list."

I wasn't listening anymore, however. Well, not really. I'm on the kill list of so many spooks, the whole thing has really gotten old.

"Jesse," I said, my gaze fastened on the front of his jeans. "Is it my imagination, or are you *overly* glad to see me?"

"I have no idea what you're talking about, Susannah. If this boy wants to kill you—or even if he only wants to kill this other boy, Zack—we should go now, and try to stop him."

"Yeah, in a minute. Jesse, what's in your pocket?"

His hand went instinctively to the hard lump I'd noticed—and been mistaking for something else all night. His expression turned unreadable—as it always did when the subject changed to something he didn't want to discuss, like what being dead had been like, or his predilection for the musical stylings of Nicki Minaj—and he dropped his hand away.

"It's nothing. We need to go. Get your coat."

"Jesse, that is *not* nothing. I thought you were glad to see me, but I think I was sadly mistaken. Is that a gun in your pocket?"

He threw me a sour glance. "No, Susannah, I do not have a gun in my pocket. Doctors swear an oath to protect human life, not take it." Then his brown-eyed gaze grew hard. "Well, unless it's a human who's already dead, and is trying to harm my girlfriend. Now can we go?"

"No, we cannot." I took a step forward.

Jesse's pretty fast, what with the whole having-walked-in-the-valley-of-the-shadow-of-death thing.

But with all the laps I swim in the campus pool (and paranormal butts I have to kick), I'm faster. I had one finger through a belt loop of his jeans (to hold him still) and another down his pocket more quickly than he could say, "Good morning, ma'am" (a frustrating habit of his of which I've tried to cure him. No one wants to be called *ma'am.* The first time he said it to my mom, I thought she was going to have a coronary).

"Susannah," he cried, struggling against me—or more like against himself. I don't think he could decide whether he was more outraged or delighted to find my hand down his pants pocket.

But then when I cried, "Aha! Got it!" and withdrew the treasure I'd discovered from the depths of his jeans, he grew very still. I don't know which one of us was more mortified when I saw what it was.

Because of course it wasn't a gun.

It was a ring box.

Seis

JESSE WAS THE first to recover himself.

"Well, I hope you're satisfied, Miss Simon," he said, and nimbly snatched the box from my hand, then stuffed it back into his pocket.

I was too emotional to say anything. I was experiencing many "feels" as the kids on Tumblr—my computer-savvy friend CeeCee has told me about it—often say. I felt panic and joy and shame over my behavior, but also exultant over the fact that the ring box wasn't large enough to have caused *all* the hardness I'd felt against me while we'd been making out earlier. So I'd been right: he *had* been happy to see me.

"But Jesse," I said, when I finally found my voice. "I thought we'd agreed we were going to wait until we were both finished with our education, and *then* get married, because of your nineteenth-century macho man bullshit idea that you have to support me. Which of course is ridiculous since I fully intend to support myself. And you."

"Yes," he said, with forced patience. He hated it when I brought up the part about how I was going to support him, which is why I brought it up as often as possible. It's important to keep your romantic partner on their toes. "But we could still get engaged."

"*Engaged?*" My voice broke on the word. "Jesse, no one our age gets *engaged*. They live together first, to see how things are going to work out, then—"

"We already did that, Susannah," he reminded me matter-of-factly. "And I think you'll agree that things 'worked out' beneficially for both of us."

"Yes, but . . ." I struggled to put into words what I was feeling. The difficulty was that I didn't know what I was feeling.

Of course Jesse and I had discussed the fact that we were going to get married someday. We didn't have one of those dumb relationships you read about in books where they can't talk about having a future together because one person can't commit due to his abusive past. Jesse had had the most abusive past you could imagine, and all he wanted to do now was move forward from it. We'd both nearly *died* for one another. We'd both given each other up so the other could live. I'd definitely known this was coming.

I just didn't think this would be coming *now*. Tonight.

And that I'd have ruined it by pulling the ring out of my boyfriend's pants moments before, ruining the surprise.

"Can we just pretend that didn't happen?" I asked. "I mean the thing where I pulled that out of your pocket?"

"Gladly," he said, tersely. "But people our age do get engaged, Susannah. You just told me that this Mark fellow—"

"He was in *the twelfth grade*, and look what happened to him!"

"What about your stepbrother?" Jesse demanded. "He's your age, and he's married."

"If you mean Brad, who impregnated his girlfriend with triplets soon after high school graduation because they neglected to use birth control, I don't know that they're the best example."

I'd never really had high expectations for my stepbrother Brad, to whom I'd always mentally referred as Dopey.

But I'd never in a million years thought I'd live to see him pushing around a stroller with three angel-faced toddler girls in it, calling him Daddy (and me Auntie Suze).

Yet that had not only happened, it happened *regularly*. Weirder still, Brad was now one of the happiest individuals I knew, and almost bearable to be around. It was too bad about his sourpuss troll of a wife.

"We're not Brad and Debbie," Jesse said from between gritted teeth.

"Uh, no, we are not," I said. "I've been on the pill for four years just in case you ever break that abstinence-until-marriage vow of yours because I don't want babies—let alone triplets—until I've at least got my master's degree."

"And I appreciate that," Jesse said. "But I'm also not like this spirit of yours, who you think was only trying to trap his girlfriend into staying true to him while she was away at school."

"Well," I said, "that's a relief. But then, I never thought you were—"

"But I *am* a man, Susannah," he went on, pulling me toward him with one hand while extracting the ring box from his pocket with another.

"Well, that is abundantly clear." I had a front row seat to the button fly of his jeans, and now that his pockets were empty, I could tell that he was, indeed, still glad to see me. "Abundantly."

"And I'm not going to be told what to do."

"When have I *ever* told you what to—?"

"Every minute of every day since the moment I met you. Even now, you're telling me not to ask you to marry me."

"Well, I just think the timing is wrong. Asking a girl to marry you on Valentine's Day is very clichéd. And asking her in her dorm room *in the Virgin Vault* is even worse."

"Well, I would have done it at sunset on the beach," he said, with a crooked smile, "if you hadn't been off causing a freak paranormal weather phenomenon."

"Oh, right. Blame it on me. It's all my fault. It didn't have anything to do with that kid in the cemetery."

"That's exactly my point. If two *high school kids* can get engaged, Susannah, why can't—"

I flung my hands over my ears. I knew I was acting like a freak, but then again, I am a freak. A bona fide

biological freak who can see ghosts and was getting proposed to—only not, because I'd ruined it, in the way I
ruin everything—by a former one.

"Stop talking about them," I said, my hands still over
my ears. "And where did you even get that?" I nodded
toward the hand that was holding the ring. He'd flipped
open the lid to give me close-up view of what I was missing. It was yellow gold—not my style, but still very pretty—
with filigree along either side of a not-unsizable center
diamond. Very retro, but probably worth a fortune.

Not that its cost had anything to do with the fact that
I suddenly wanted to throw up.

"You don't have any money," I went on. Then I lowered my hands with a gasp. "Jesse! You didn't spend all
your fellowship money on a ring for me, did you?"

"No, I didn't," he said. "Because I'm not stupid. This
ring has been in my family for generations. It was my
mother's. And before that, my grandmother's. Now I'm
hoping it will be yours . . . if you'd act like a lady for five
seconds and let me propose properly, and put it on your
finger."

I stared at him. How could he have his mother's ring?
I knew everything about him, but I'd never known this.

Well, not *everything*, of course. Not the things I most
wanted to know, like what he looked like naked, or even
what he looked like sleeping—unconscious, maybe, but
not asleep. After I'd saved him from ever having been
murdered in the first place (long story, and another one
of our secrets), Father Dominic had forged a few records
to help accelerate Jesse's educational process, and he'd

managed to skip four years of college. When you've got nothing to do for nearly two hundred years but haunt the room you'd died in during a previous life, you end up reading a lot of books. Most of the books Jesse read were medical journals. He passed the MCATs with one of the highest scores in California state history, and had schools falling all over themselves, offering him scholarships.

And now he was offering me his mother's ring, and I was offering him attitude.

What was wrong with me?

"Not now, all right?" I said, breaking free of his embrace. "Right now we have more important things to do. We have to go keep one ghost from turning a kid into another ghost, remember? And possibly me, too. So let's go do it, and talk about this later."

He frowned as I began to buzz around the room, gathering my ghost-busting material. "Susannah, did I do something wrong?"

"You? What could you *possibly* have done wrong?"

"That's what I'm asking you. *Querida*, are you *blushing*?"

"Of course not." My cheeks were hot as fire. But I couldn't tell him why, because I didn't know why. "Well, okay, maybe I am. I just can't deal with this right now."

"Can't deal with what right now? The man who loves you asking you to spend the rest of your life with him?"

"Not that. That part's a given. I mean, I'd kill you if you didn't."

"Is this about your mother?" he asked, flipping the ring box closed as I shoved my cell phone into a bowl of uncooked rice I keep on my bookshelf for just such emergencies. "Is this about how she wanted us to date other people while we were at different schools? Are you regretting that you didn't take her advice? Or—" His voice grew oddly still. "Did you take her advice? Is that where you really were tonight?"

"God, Jesse, of course not!" I exploded. "What do you think, that I made up this elaborate story about the kid in the cemetery so you wouldn't find out I'm cheating on you with some dumb frat boy? Are you *kidding* me?"

Jesse looked thoughtful. "I was thinking of a teaching assistant. I couldn't see you with a fraternity boy. You'd probably only scare them."

I grabbed my messenger bag. "Thanks for the compliment. Now we should probably go. Is your phone charged? I need you to check and see if there's a local address listed for a family under the name of Farhat. Please, God, there can't be more than one."

"Or do you think I'm trying to trap you the way the dead boy did his girlfriend because I don't know where I'm going to be for my residency next year?" he mused. "We could be even farther apart than we are now. But I swear that's not what this is about. I'm confident that wherever I end up, we'll work it out."

"Oh, my God, Jesse, I know." I reached for the vodka and cranberry Lauren had given me. Now that Jesse was here, he could drive. He's a better driver than I am—which is disturbing, considering I've had a license longer than he had—and I needed the liquid courage. For what we were about to do, and, well, for other things.

"Then is it nerves about telling your mother and step-father our plans?" he asked. "If this was the 1850s—and I'm glad it's not, because I'm grateful for vaccines and antibiotics—I'd be asking Andy's permission to marry you." He ignored the choking sound I made, which had nothing to do with the drink I was chugging. "I'm not going to, not only because I understand that would be—what did it you call it again? Oh, yes— ridiculously chau-vinistic, but because you obviously seem to have some kind of issue about the idea of our getting engaged right now. That's fine. I can wait. But I do think we should con-sider telling your parents the truth about how we met and who I really am and how you can actually see the undead. It's a bad idea to start a marriage with a lie —"

"Oh, my God, no!" I burst out—though not loudly enough to draw the attention of my suite mates, who for all I knew were listening at the door. I wouldn't put it past them. Some of them had never been on dates before, and so were extremely curious about them. "Are you insane? I can't tell my mom any of that stuff, let alone Andy. It would blow their tiny little minds. They'll think we were in a cult, or something."

"Having the gift of second sight is hardly the same as being in a cult, Susannah."

"You know my mother. She's a reporter. And now she's the executive producer of Andy's show. She only be-lieves in facts she can see."

Jesse thrust out a hand, the one holding the ring box. "Does *this* look factual enough to you, Susannah?"

I knew he was talking about the ring, but it was difficult not to notice how hard and muscular his hand looked, especially attached to that long, equally muscular arm. That was a fact my mother wouldn't be able to ignore, either. It was hard to believe that such a vibrantly masculine, stunningly attractive person, whose dark eyes practically flashed with intelligence and life, had ever been dead. Any residency program that didn't take him was insane. I was probably a fool not to have said, *Yes, Jesse, I will be Mrs. de Silva*, and slid that ring on my finger the moment I found it, so tantalizingly warm from the heat of his body.

But something still didn't feel right. Probably it was me. *I* didn't feel right.

"Um, yes," I said, swallowing. "But that isn't the point. My mom and Andy have enough to worry about with Brad and the babies and now Jake starting his own, ahem, business."

My oldest stepbrother, Jake—whose only career aspiration upon high school graduation appeared to be a full-time pizza delivery position—had surprised us all by parlaying his pizza delivery earnings not into the Camaro of which he'd always dreamed, but into the purchase of a plot of land in Salinas.

A short while later, he opened a storefront in Carmel Valley that dispensed not pizza, but another item of which college students in particular are fond of imbibing late at night. Only one needed a medical prescription to purchase this particular item in the state of California.

I found this business venture of Jake's highly entrepreneurial, yet at the same time ironic, considering I'd privately nicknamed him Sleepy, since he'd seemed to go through life with his eyes half closed. If only I'd known the real reason why.

Well, we all know now.

Jake's medical marijuana dispensary—the only one in the tri-county region—did amazing business, and he was rapidly becoming one of the wealthiest business owners in the area. He'd bought a cool little house in the Valley and, whether out of generosity of spirit or because he genuinely liked him, convinced Jesse to move into the spare bedroom, so he'd have a place to stay when he came home from school on breaks.

"You can't keep stayin' with that old dude when you're here, man," was how Jake put it. By "old dude," he meant Father Dominic. "No one should live in a monastery, unless they're a priest. And you're no priest, man. I've seen the way you look at my sister. No offense."

I hadn't expected Jesse to accept, especially after an invitation couched quite like that.

But either living with Father Dominic really had become more than even a believer as faithful as Jesse could stand, or he was finally ready to step into the twenty-first century, because Jesse does stay with Jake every time he's in town.

Between Jake's marijuana business venture and Brad's teenage parenthood, I would have become my parents' golden child if my youngest stepbrother, David, hadn't gotten accepted early decision to Harvard and been assigned to live in (where else?) Kirkland House.

Keeping my "gift" a secret is really hard sometimes,

but the alternative—having a cheesy reality show on the Lifetime Network where I go around telling people that their dead relative is in heaven now, smiling down at them—seems way worse.

Jesse dropped his hand and frowned at me. "Susannah, I would think our getting engaged would be *good* news, something everyone in your family would appreciate, and even celebrate. What is it that's so upsetting you about my trying to propose?"

"Nothing," I said, and grabbed my coat. "I told you. I just can't deal with it right now. Did you find the address of the probably already dead boy?"

He put the ring away and swiftly typed into his phone. For someone who despised modern technology, he was extremely good at using it. "No. It says their number and address is unlisted. These things are hopeless."

"Nothing is hopeless," I said. "You of all people should know that by now." Then I flung open the door to my dorm room.

I probably shouldn't have been surprised that all six of my suite mates were crouched outside it.

Siete

"THE FARHATS ARE Persian," said my suite mate Parisa. She was the one who was dating a guy in a motorcycle gang. If her parents found out, they'd kill her, she cheerfully informed us.

"Not literally," she explained to Jesse, who looked a little alarmed. "I'm Persian, too, you see. My mom wants me to find a nice medical student like you." She batted her thick eyelash extensions at him. "And if I could find one as cute as you, I would. But he'd have to be Persian, of course."

"I'm Spanish," Jesse said hastily. I think he was a little anxious about being surrounded by so many gorgeous women—at least, I think they're gorgeous. I know *I* am—one of whom was Persian, and all of whom had overheard our argument in my room.

He didn't have anything to be concerned about, however. My girls had his back. And mine.

"That's okay," Parisa assured him. "With hair and eyebrows like that, you could pass."

"He's taken, Par," I reminded her.

"Yeah, but maybe I could just borrow him to take home for the holidays," Parisa purred. "My mom would be so happy."

"Or you could just quit dating a gangbanger who sexually abuses women, deals drugs, and traffics stolen goods," suggested Valentina, the lesbian women's studies major. "Or would that interfere with your plan to get back at your dad for not buying you that BMW you wanted for high school graduation?"

Parisa smiled and shrugged her slinky shoulders. "It was a Porsche. And Ray's not as bad as his friends. Besides, he's got a really big"—she glanced at Jesse, saw my warning glance, and smiled harder—"*motorcycle*."

Valentina rolled her eyes and poured herself another V and C. We'd all agreed this is the best cocktail, because it not only tastes good, but the cranberry juice allegedly helps ward off urinary tract infections.

"Getting back to the subject at hand," I said, with a cough. "You say the Farhats live over in Carmel?"

"Right. There's a really big Persian community there." Parisa handed me the address on a piece of her Pomeranian puppy–shaped notepad paper. "Well, not as big as in Los Angeles, but, like, big enough." She explained to Jesse, as if he were a child, "Most people think of carpets or kittens when they hear the word Persian, but we're actually an ethnic group from north of the Persian Gulf."

Jesse smiled at her politely. "Yes, I know. Thank you for clarifying that, though."

"Oh," she gushed. "Not a problem."

I tapped her on the shoulder. "So do you know what the deal is with this Zack kid?"

"Yeah, totally. It's Zakaria, not Zack. I mean, his Westernized name is Zack, but in Persian it's Zakaria. His parents are friends with my parents, and I've been to their house a few times. That kid is so spoiled—I mean, that's true of a lot Persian kids, but he's even more spoiled than most because he's the youngest, and his family is, like, *mega* rich. His dad's a heart surgeon. And they're super good friends with the Ahmadis, the parents of that girl who died last month. I think they were even distantly related—second cousins, or something. I was at the funeral, and Zakaria's mom was bawling her eyes out. Well, we all were, because it was so sad. Jasmin was just a kid, and some guy killed her. How does that even happen?"

"Ask your boyfriend," Valentina suggested.

Parisa ignored her. "But Mrs. Farhat was especially upset. And Zakaria, too. He kept his sunglasses on the whole time so no one could see how red his eyes were."

"Aw," said Melodia. She was the girl whose family didn't allow her to speak to men outside of her religion. Obviously, this was not a rule she actually followed when her family was not around. "That's so sad."

Jesse and I exchanged glances. I knew what he was thinking. Zack had kept his glasses on to hide the fact that his eyes were red from crying . . . or something else.

"So do you know what kind of car this Zack kid owns?" I asked Parisa.

"What kind *doesn't* he own? Last time I was there, he had, like, three cars . . . a Jeep for the beach, a Beamer for school, and a pickup truck for whatever the hell kids like that do with pickup trucks."

Kill girls who aren't interested in them, apparently.

"Thanks, Par," I said, stuffing the address in the pocket of my jacket. "This is a huge help."

"I don't understand why you guys are going over there *now*," Lauren, the witch, said. "Not that I'm ungrateful to the mother goddess, because we need the rain, but there are flash flood warnings everywhere, and they're advising people to stay off the roads."

"Yeah," Melodia said. "This is a good night to stay *in*, not go out."

I couldn't tell how much of this was genuine concern on their parts, or a desire for us to stick around so they could listen some more through the door, and hear the drama through to the end. I wasn't sure how much they'd already learned. Not enough, evidently, to know that I could speak to the dead, but enough to know that Jesse and I were on the outs for some reason.

I understood—and could even sympathize with and appreciate—their interest. Real-life drama is infinitely preferable to most of what we see on TV. That stuff is so unbelievable.

I wasn't going to give them the satisfaction, however, for a variety of reasons. We had a soul to save, not to mention a life.

"Sorry, girls," I said. "Jesse's really worried about this kid. What disease was it that you think he might have come into contact with in your ER? Ebola?"

Jesse rolled his eyes heavenward. He was always getting on my back about my alleged inability to lie convincingly, but my sociology prof says that studies show, the bigger the lie, the harder people will fall for it, because most human beings believe no one would ever tell an enormous whopper to their face (which is why they fall so easily into the clutches of corrupt politicians, kitchen contractors, and sleazy boyfriends).

"It's probably only a mild case of salmonella, Susannah," Jesse said. "And it was from the hospital cafeteria, not the ER. Still, it's important we question him and the rest of his family immediately. These things have a way of spreading if proper precautions aren't taken."

"I thought you were here to take Susannah out for dinner for Valentine's Day," Ashley said, suspiciously. Being a thief, she had sharper hearing than the others. She needed it for her trade. And since she was a criminal justice major, she was going to need it for her future career, as well.

"Well, I thought I'd combine work with pleasure," Jesse said, assuming a properly shameful expression. "I suppose you caught me, Ashley."

She grinned and patted him on the shoulder. "Sorry about that, Jess. Didn't mean to put you on the spot there."

That's when I noticed an unfamiliar flash of green on her wrist. Looking more closely, I saw that she was wearing an emerald and diamond tennis bracelet with white gold links. It looked expensive.

An emerald and diamond tennis bracelet? Where had Ashley—who'd had to pawn all her jewelry to pay off the criminal fines she'd accrued during the height of her disorder—gotten hold of such an expensive piece of jewelry?

Then I remembered the bulky envelope I'd stuffed into my messenger bag.

Swiftly, I opened the bag and pulled out the envelope. It had been opened and re-sealed—cleverly, so that it would have been difficult to tell if I hadn't already been suspicious. But I probably would have observed it earlier if I'd taken half a second to look.

Now I slid open the envelope and found inside it only an empty jewelry box—one of those beautifully wrapped ones that come from the high-end jewelry stores, with the wide silk ribbon and certificate of authenticity—and a card.

The card was tacky, a mass-produced Valentine's Day card, the kind Jesse had said I was too good for, in the shape of a heart, with a cupid on it, aiming an arrow at the viewer. *You Slay Me*, it said, in a goofy font.

When I opened it, Paul had written, in his atrocious handwriting (he was used to typing, texting, and gaming, not writing with a pen, like Jesse):

I know you'll hate this, but I saw them (both the card and bracelet), and thought of you. The emeralds match your eyes (I know, I'm getting sentimental in my old age, aren't I?) and you slayed me long ago.

I know your first impulse is going to be to send the bracelet back, but why? That undead cholo boyfriend of yours can't afford to get you anything nice for Valentine's Day, so just pretend it's from him. It can be our little secret, like the other little secrets we have from him ;-)

> *Love always,*
> *Paul*

I lifted my gaze—not to look at anything in particular, only because I couldn't stare at those words for a second longer—and found Ashley looking in my direction, her face bright red. She must have seen what I was doing, noticed my expression, and thought my anger was targeted at her as the only likely suspect for filching the gift that should have been inside the package.

She thrust the wrist encircled by the bracelet behind her back, then, looking even more sheepish, brought it out again, and pointed to it.

Sorry, she mouthed guiltily, looking anguished. *I'll give it back.*

I nearly laughed out loud. *Yes,* I mouthed back. *You will.*

But only so I could mail the bracelet back to Paul, with a note advising him that he could take both it and his Valentine and stuff it up his—

"Are you ready to go?" Jesse asked. Then he noticed the card in my hand. "What's that?"

"Oh," I said, and shoved everything—the card, envelope, and empty jewelry box—into a nearby pedal bin. "Nothing."

Jesse seemed bemused as he watched me try to close the lid of the trash bin. I might have been hitting it a little more violently than necessary. "It doesn't look like nothing."

"Trust me, it is." The lid finally went down and stayed down. I straightened. "And yes, I'm ready. Let's go."

Ocho

"IT LOOKS LIKE the Farhats are having a party."

"What?"

Jesse's voice startled me. I'd become hypnotized by the sound of the wipers against the windshield as we'd navigated our way through the flooded streets of Carmel-by-the-Sea, ruminating on how in the course of one evening, I'd had funerary planters thrown at me, ruined a perfectly good marriage proposal, been stalked by an ex, and caused a catastrophic weather event in Northern California.

Surprisingly, this wasn't the worst Valentine's Day of my life.

"I said, it looks like the Farhats are having a party."

It did, actually. The house at the address Parisa had given us was on a seaside road so exclusive, the homes there listed in the high seven figures (when they went on sale at all, which was rarely). The Farhats' sprawling place was lit up as brightly as a toy store on Christmas Eve, and bouquets of heart-shaped, helium-filled balloons—now looking a bit bedraggled in the rain—dotted the fence, punctuating the line of cars all down the long driveway, stretching out onto the street.

Evidently the Farhats weren't going to let the weather—or the death of a beloved teenage cousin—spoil their good time.

"Good," I said. "We can go in like we were invited. Too bad we didn't bring that bottle of sparkling wine. It would have been a nice hostess gift, to throw them off."

Jesse pulled into a space as close as he could get to the house, though we were still going to be soaked as we made our way in.

"That's one of the many things I love about you, Susannah," he said. "You're always so polite to the parents of the kids you've unintentionally set up to be murdered."

"It's just the way I was raised."

I checked my reflection in the sun visor's vanity mirror, and saw that my eyeliner, lip gloss, and hair were in order, though they'd soon be ruined by the rain, despite the fact that there was an umbrella in the backseat, and I had every intention of using it. This wasn't that kind of rain. It was the mean, sideways-slanting kind.

"Shall we?" I asked.

"Let's."

Bursting into parties to which I wasn't invited—but acting as if I had every right in the world to be there—is another one of my many gifts. It's basically all about confidence—and having the right shoes, of course. If you have the right shoes, you can do anything.

And I had on my favorite shoes, a pair of black leather platform boots with a steel-reinforced toe and chunky heel that basically screamed, *This girl is not to be messed with*. I don't know why Mark Rodgers hadn't been intimidated.

It helped also that I walked into the Farhats party with Jesse at my side. He's so tall and handsome and—it must be admitted—*otherworldly looking*, despite living in this world now, people can't help staring and wondering if they've seen him before. (They have. He looks just like every mid-nineteenth century romantic Spanish poet or soldier or ship captain who died tragically just after having his portrait painted by some artist who was besotted with him. Everyone's seen pictures like these hanging in museums or in some mansion on a show on PBS or something).

Tonight was no different. A dark-haired lady wearing a flowy pantsuit and a lot of heavy gold jewelry came hurrying over to us when we blew through the door—literally, we were blown through the door by the gusting wind—and cried, "Why, hello! You made it!"

"Yes, we made it," I said, shrugging out of my leather jacket and handing it to the person who was hovering nearby in black pants, white shirt, and a black vest and bow tie . . . the ubiquitous uniform in Carmel for hired party waitstaff.

I was relieved to see that, beyond the foyer, the party was in full swing. The aggressively modern home was crowded with well-dressed middle-aged people all holding wineglasses and chattering as loudly as possible so that they could hear one another over the sound of the pounding rain on the roof, the roar of the surf beyond the sliding glass doors leading to the pool, and the over-loud tinkling of the baby grand in the corner, at which a hired professional was crooning how "s'wonderful" and "s'marvelous" it was that we should care for him.

In one swift glance, I recognized Carmel's mayor, police chief, and chief prosecutor, all schmoozing it up with their spouses.

If a crazed, murderous spirit had burst in and at-tempted to kill the Farhats' son any time in the past hour, I doubted any of them would still be there, let alone be in such a party mood—if they'd even noticed, of course. Non-Compliant Deceased Persons don't always make their presence known as obviously as Mark had at the cemetery.

Then again, I was fairly certain he hadn't gotten the sweet revenge he was seeking, or the storm outside would have already abated.

And it seemed as if Zack might be home, since Jesse and I had spotted the "Beamer" and Jeep that Parisa had described, along with an F150 pickup that looked like it might belong to a teenager—the bed was jacked up away from the enormous wheels, and there was a large sticker of a snorting bull (the mascot of one of area's high school football teams) in the back windshield—parked close to the home.

A close examination of the truck (as close as we could make in the dark during a violent rainstorm) re-vealed nothing to show that it might have been involved

in a vehicular manslaughter near Big Sur last month . . .
unless the kid was friends with an extremely talented
(and quick) auto repair person.

True, he could have called a friend to come pick
him up for the night. It was possible he and his "friend
group"—that's what they called them now, instead of
cliques—had gone to the movies or something.

But would his parents really have let him go out in
weather like this?

"It was touch and go there for a while," I rattled on
with the hostess, scanning the high-ceilinged room for
any sign of someone who might be Zack's age. But all I
could see were more heart-shaped, helium-filled balloons,
along with a banner that said THANK YOU DONORS! with
red hearts all over it. I had no idea what that was about,
and didn't care. "Especially on Scenic Road—you would
not believe the waves—I don't blame those people for
sandbagging their driveways. But we're here!"

The lady—she was older, with such gorgeous highlights that I envied her—had to be Mrs. Farhat. She radi-
ated prideful home ownership.

"Wonderful!" she said. "The more the merrier. You
know, we give this party every year, and every year, we
never fail to be pleased with the turnout, despite it being
Valentine's Day. Some people think it's a bit morbid, but
heart disease, is, after all—"

"—the number one cause of death in the world," Jesse
finished for her, handing his own coat and our dripping
umbrella to the waitperson. "Actually, I think it's very
clever of you to hold a fund-raiser for coronary disease on

Valentine's Day, Mrs. Farhat. More women die annually of cardiovascular diseases than from all forms of cancer combined."

"Why, yes," Mrs. Farhat said, instantly charmed as Jesse took the hand she'd extended and shook it. "Yes, I know. My mother died of heart disease. By the time we found out how sick she was, it was too late for even my husband to help her. I've been trying to raise awareness ever since. Thank you. And who might you be?"

"Hector de Silva," he said, gazing deeply into her eyes. "Dr. Hector de Silva."

Her expression couldn't have lit up more if he'd said his name was Bond. James Bond.

"A doctor?" she said, taking his arm. "Why haven't we met before? Surely you're not with the hospital here, or I'd know you—"

"No, not here," he said. "Not yet, anyway. But I hope to be, someday."

"Someday!" Mrs. Farhat was already steering him away from me, into the sunken living room. "With hands like yours, young man, you could work anywhere, trust me. I can tell, I know doctors. My husband is a cardiac surgeon. Let me introduce you to him. Rashid. Rashid!"

Jesse was soon sucked up into a crowd of admirers, just as I'd hoped he would be. He was a big boy, and would be able to handle himself. In the meantime, I had some snooping to do.

"Crudité?" a waitperson asked as she passed me while holding a tray of decoratively carved raw vegetables. "They're heart healthy."

"Uh," I said. "Sure." I lifted a heart-shaped radish and shoved it into my mouth. I'm not the biggest fan of raw vegetables—except when shredded onto a taco—but this one was surprisingly good. "Thanks. Can you tell me where the bathroom is?"

"Of course." The girl pointed down the hall. "To the left. You can't miss it."

"Thanks. Oh, hey, do you know if the Farhats' son, Zack, is here tonight? A friend of his asked me to say hello."

The girl smiled in a friendly way, anxious to be helpful. "Yes, he's here. He was hanging out in the kitchen a while ago. I think he took some food up to his room." Her gaze went toward the showy curved staircase across the foyer from the front door, signaling to me where I could find Zack's room, though I doubt she'd done it on purpose. "Well, not this food. He microwaved a pizza."

"Thank you so much," I said, and took another radish. "Yum. These are just so delicious."

"Consuming fruits and vegetables, combined with regular physical activity, and avoiding harmful use of alcohol and tobacco products, has been shown to reduce the risk of cardiovascular disease," she said, clearly because she'd been asked to by the hostess.

"Wow," I said. "Great. Thanks."

"You're welcome!" She moved on to her next victim, I mean guest, and I moved toward the staircase, acting like I had every right to be heading to the second floor. The only way you're going to get caught snooping is if your performance while doing it lacks confidence. If anyone walks in on you while you're somewhere you shouldn't be, just act angry. It's *their* fault you're in the wrong place, because you were told (by someone else) that that's where you were supposed to be. How were you supposed to know that person was wrong?

Seriously. It works (almost) every time.

It only took me four rooms (two more than usual) before I found Zack. He hadn't even bothered to lock the door, the idiot.

"Really?" I said, when I walked in and discovered him sitting up in bed in front of a large plasma-screen television, playing video games and vaping. "I could have been anyone—your mother, your father, the police chief. He's downstairs, you know. Is it really wise of you to be partaking at the current time?"

Zack peered at me through weed-reddened eyes. "This is e-juice. Who the hell are you, and what do you want?"

"That is not e-juice, and as a minor, you better have a prescription for it *and* your parents' permission. Otherwise you're in violation of California health and safety code and could lose the right to operate your vehicle. *All* your vehicles."

This information caused him to lower the e-cigarette and swallow, hard.

"My name is Suze Simon," I went on. "And as much as I can't believe I'm saying this, I'm here to rescue you. Now get up, before Mark Rodgers comes in here and kills you."

Nueve

IF I HADN'T believed Mark's version of what had happened that night on Rocky Creek Bridge, I did when I saw the expression that flashed across Zack Farhat's face when I said Mark was coming to kill him.

Sheer panic. For a second, he lowered his hands to the king-sized mattress and began to push himself up from in front of the plasma screen, as if to go with me.

Never had I seen a more guilty-looking individual, someone who'd known he'd done wrong and had been expecting what was coming to him. Zack—a strong, dark, handsome boy—was accepting his fate like a man.

Well, this is good, I thought. *Not what I was expecting, but good . . . the first good thing to happen all day, as a matter of fact. Maybe things are starting to go my way.*

Of course I thought too soon. It didn't last. Why would it?

Because a split second later, Zack seemed to realize

something through his drug-induced haze, and froze. The panic left, and was replaced by a look I recognized, because I'd seen it before on the faces of a hundred guys just like him.

Nope. Never mind. No win for Suze. This guy thought he was smarter than me. He thought he was smarter than everyone.

Well, why not? He'd already killed two people and gotten away with it. All he had to do was stick with his story, and he was home free.

Or so he thought.

He lowered himself back against his bed.

"Wait," he said, drawing the word out so that it had about five syllables, in true stoner form. "Mark can't be coming here to kill me. He's dead."

"You're right about the last part," I said. "Not so right about the first. Mark's dead, but he's not very happy with you for killing him, and Jasmin, too. See, that's why minors aren't supposed to smoke that stuff unless they're under a licensed physician's care. It makes them forgetful." I hit him in the forehead with the flat of my hand on the word *forgetful*. "And also stupid." I hit him again on the word *stupid*.

"Ow." He ducked and crawled to the far side of the bed so he'd be out of my reach. "Stop that. What are you talking about? What makes you think I had anything to do with—?"

"The deaths of Mark Rodgers and Jasmin Ahmadi? Oh, gosh, Zack, I don't know. Maybe *that*?"

I pointed to a far wall of his room, opposite a pair of

French doors that led out to a balcony overlooking the Pacific Ocean (which for once didn't look so pacified, thanks to the storm). Taped to the wall were dozens—maybe even a hundred—photos of Jasmin, including the one from her headstone, which must have been one of her senior photos, since there were other equally posed photos of her in the same outfit, smiling confidently into the camera.

Only instead of sending these photos out with her graduation announcements, her grieving family had apparently sent them to her friends and family with an announcement of her death.

Zack had artfully arranged these particular photos in a large heart shape around a single photo of the two of them arm-in-arm from what appeared to have been a Halloween party, since he was dressed as a tiger and she a bunny rabbit (I estimated it was a party circa fourth grade, possibly the last time Jasmin had willingly allowed herself to be photographed beside him, at least on non-digital film).

Beneath this display Zack had lit a number of votive candles on a small table, and also laid out a copy of what appeared to be their school yearbook, open to a page showing Jasmin's prowess on the track team.

Oh, yeah. This guy wasn't a creeper at all.

"If that's not a shrine," I said, "I don't know what is."

"So?" Zack looked sullen. "What's so weird about that? She was my cousin, and she died. That's what people do when someone they love dies."

"Oh, yeah? How much did you love her, Zack? Enough

to fly into a jealous rage when she started seeing someone else?"

That got to him. His gaze darkened, and his lower jaw began to jut out a little. I think he was trying to look manly, but that was a little difficult for a kid wearing so many gold necklaces . . . especially one playing video games. He'd reached for the remote again.

"Get out of my room," he said, his gaze fastened to the screen. "I don't even know who you are. And I sure as hell don't know what you're talking about."

"I think you do know what I'm talking about, Zack. You followed them the night of the accident. You followed them to the restaurant, saw Mark propose, and saw her say yes."

He shrugged, still staring at the screen. The sounds of the tortured deaths he was causing were loud enough nearly to drown out the rain outside.

"Nice try, lady," he said. "Everyone in the restaurant saw that. It was on the news."

"What wasn't on the news was what happened after Mark and Jasmin left the restaurant," I said. "How you followed them out of the parking lot in your—what did Mark call it? Oh yes. Your souped-up monster truck—then turned your brights on, riding their tail until you forced them into that cliff off Rocky Creek Bridge, because the other lane was closed."

That got his attention. His fingers stilled on the game console. His gaze flicked uneasily toward me.

"That . . . that isn't true." But the unsteadiness of his voice—and what he said next—proved otherwise. "And even if it was—which it isn't—there weren't any witnesses. Mark's dead. So is Jasmin. Mark can't do anything to me because he's dead."

It was at that moment that the French doors to the balcony burst open with an explosive crash.

Diez

BLOWN WIDE BY a sudden gust of gale-force wind, the open balcony doors allowed rain and leaves to fly across the room.

The gale detached most of Jasmin's photos from the wall of the shrine on the opposite wall, and doused the flames in the votive candles, plunging the room into darkness, except for the glow of the plasma screen. The gauzy white curtains that hung from a rod above the doors streamed like the yearning arms of a mother reaching for her long-lost child.

Zack let out an expletive, threw down the game console, and leaped from his bed, looking terrified.

I didn't blame him. I wasn't feeling particularly calm myself . . . and it was my job to *expect* this kind of thing.

"See, Zack?" I said, shouting to be heard over the roar of the storm outside and the banging of the French doors as the wind continued to suck them open and then closed again. "I told you. Mark is pissed."

As if to stress my point, a flash of lightning filled the sky outside, striking so close that it turned the room from midnight dark to bright as day and then back again, all in the blink of an eye . . . then caused the television to short out, showering the area where Zack had been sitting on the bed seconds before in an explosion of colorful sparks. The thunderous boom that followed was strong enough to shake the entire house.

"Holy shit," Zack cried, sinking into a ball on the floor and cradling his head against his knees. "I didn't mean it. Oh, my God, I didn't mean to do it. I didn't mean for it to happen that way!"

The second he admitted it, the storm stopped. As if someone had pulled a switch, the French doors stopped banging, and the wind and rain and debris that had been streaming through them died away, leaving behind only the smell of ocean brine and the earthy odor of petrichor, the fragrance released from soil after it's gone too long without rain. The gauzy white curtains on either side of the balcony doors hung limp, like abandoned rag dolls.

"Oh, my God," Zack sobbed softly into his knees. "Oh, my God. Thank God."

The thing was, he thought he was safe now. And why wouldn't he? The storm was over.

I knew, however, that it had only just begun.

Because I could see what Zack couldn't. And that was that he and I weren't alone in that dark bedroom. Standing next to one of those gauzy white curtains was a figure, a dark figure dressed all in black, even down to the frames of his eyeglasses. He was staring at Zack's crumpled, sobbing form.

And there wasn't the slightest hint of pity in his gaze.

"What should I do to him?" Mark asked me in an emotionless voice.

"Nothing," I said. "You've done enough already. Leave him alone, Mark. Like I told you in the cemetery, it will only make things worse for you if you do anything to him. He admitted it. I'll make sure justice is served."

"Justice," Mark said, with a sneer. "What a stupid, meaningless word. Justice isn't going to bring her back. Or me."

"I know. But he'll get what he deserves."

"No," Mark said. There was emotion in his voice now. It was scorn. "He won't. You watch. He won't. The rich never do."

I was afraid Mark was right. Where was the proof? That was the problem. There was no proof.

But I tried to lie, for Mark's sake.

"His mother's a good person," I said. "I don't know about his dad, but I think he's all right, too. They're both trying to help others. When they find out the dangerous person their son really is, they'll make sure he's removed from society."

Mark let out a bitter laugh. "Yeah," he said. "Sure. That will happen."

Zack lifted his head and stared at me through eyelids that were even more red-rimmed than before. "Who the *hell* are you talking to, lady?"

"Mark," I replied, simply. I leaned down to adjust my boots. I had a feeling I was going to need them in a few minutes. "He's here to kill you. I was just telling him that isn't going to be necessary. You're going to put yourself away for what you did to him and Jasmin."

Zack wiped his eyes, his expression growing steelier by the second. "The hell I am."

"Oh, yes," I said, doing a few neck rolls. "You are. You're a danger to yourself, Zack, but mostly you're a danger to others."

"You're full of shit," was Zack's witty reply.

"That's entirely possible," I said, pushing up my sleeves. "But your tendency toward violence; your blatant disregard for the law; your obvious disdain for the rights and feelings of anyone besides yourself; but most of all your complete and total lack of remorse or guilt about your actions—you were only crying just now because you were sorry you got caught, not sorry for what you did—leads me to believe that you're a full-on sociopath. Maybe even a psychopath." I shrugged. "I don't know. I don't have my degree yet, so I can't guarantee which for sure. But do you know what I can guarantee? You are going down for the murders of Mark Rodgers and Jasmin Ahmadi. The only question is, do you want it to be the hard way? Or the easy way?"

His only response was a grunt. He'd lowered his brows into a scowl, apparently not caring for my calling him a psychopath even though all evidence pointed to this being the truth. This became especially obvious when his next move was to rise from the floor and come at me like a defensive tackle—which, for all I knew, could have been the position he played on the school team, though I hadn't seen any trophies or sports paraphernalia in his room.

Then he rammed me in the gut with his shoulder with so much force, the two of us went flying into his bookshelf.

It wasn't like I hadn't been ready for something like this. In my line of work, I get hit a lot. Father Dominic despairs of what he calls my "punch first, ask questions later" technique of Non-Compliant Deceased Person mediation.

But generally the people with whom I engage in fisticuffs are, in fact, deceased. It was a bit unusual for me to be body slammed by a living, breathing boy who had just informed me (in his own way) that he was not a danger to others.

"This isn't doing a whole lot to prove to me that you have non-violent tendencies," I said to Zack as he lay on top of me amid the rubble that had once been his bookshelf.

Or I tried to say it. What came out wasn't anything as coherent, since he'd knocked all the breath from me—and probably some of the radishes I'd eaten earlier, as well. I was afraid to look.

I became aware of a painful throbbing in my side that worsened every time I moved. Oh, great.

Zack didn't seem at all troubled by our hard landing. He rose up on one hand and lifted his other in a fist—a fist I noticed was sizable enough to do a great deal of damage if it managed to connect with my delicate feminine features.

"I'm going to kill you," he casually informed me.

Before I could duck, a strong brown hand closed around Zack's wrist.

"Not tonight," a deep, masculine—and warmly familiar—voice said.

Once

"DIDN'T YOUR MOTHER ever warn you what can happen to young ladies who wander into young men's private bedrooms during social gatherings?" Jesse asked, as he hauled Zack Farhat off me. "It can be bad for their health."

"Oh, sure." Now that I could breathe again, I sat up and took a careful assessment of my rib bone situation. None appeared to be broken, but there were going to be bruises for sure. I wouldn't be swimming much for the next few weeks. "Blame the victim. That's what everybody does."

"I didn't mean you, *querida*," Jesse said. His dark-eyed gaze, generally so full of warmth—except, of course, when he was thinking about his time as a member of the undead—was as cold with contempt as I could ever remember seeing it, and it was focused on Zack. "I meant it can be unhealthy for the young men."

He'd flipped on the overheard lights—the electricity

seemed to be working perfectly now that the storm had passed—and I could see that he hadn't loosened his grip on Zack's wrist. In fact, now he gave it a twist, bending the boy's arm behind his back in a painful submission hold that I knew my stepbrother Brad, who was still obsessed with wrestling, would probably admire.

"Let go of me, asshole." Zack struggled against his captor, but soon found that the more he fought, the more painful Jesse's grip on him became. "Seriously, stop. That really hurts. Do you want me to call my dad? Because I will, motherfu—"

"I'm actually right here, Zakaria," said a stern voice from the doorway.

Though it was a little painful to turn my head, I glanced in that direction, and saw that a well-dressed gentleman—one I could only presume, from his horrified expression was Dr. Farhat—had come up the stairs behind Jesse, along with Zack's mother.

So had the mayor. So had the chief prosecutor. So had the police chief.

Wow. It was like the who's who of Carmel-by-the-Sea.

"We heard a terrible noise," said Mrs. Farhat, looking pale beneath her elegant makeup. She kept glancing over at me, sitting in the wreckage of her son's bookshelf. Zack still owned some of his childhood favorites—the complete Harry Potter collection, and *Good Dog Carl*. I probably looked ridiculous, sitting there among them.

But I probably hadn't looked so ridiculous when they'd opened the door and seen him crouched over me with his fist raised.

"We came up to see what in heaven's name is going on here. But I'm not so sure I want to know." Mrs. Farhat looked as horrified as her husband. "What were you doing to her, Zakaria?"

"*Me?*" Zack bleated. "Mom, you've got to be kidding me. She's the one who started it. She was trying to say that I killed Jasmin! Like *I* would ever do something like that. You know how much I loved Jasmin. We had something special. You and Dad said so yourselves. You used to say you thought we'd be married some day—"

"Oh, Zakaria." Mrs. Farhat's dark eyes were filled with compassion for her son—but also something else. Something I recognized.

Dread. She knew. She knew what was coming.

"Daddy and I were only ever joking about that, Zakaria," she went on. "It was only a little joke between us because when you were little, the two of you got along so well. But it was simply the kind of thing people say. We didn't mean anything by it—"

"Didn't mean anything by it?" Zack looked incensed. "But Jasmin and I *did* have something special. And then she had to go and spoil it by—"

"Zakaria!" Mrs. Farhat's eyes widened. The dread was turning to fear.

My heart swelled with pity for the poor woman. What must it be like, giving birth to a monster?

"I don't understand what's going on here," Dr. Farhat said. It was clear that he hadn't yet realized what his wife had—what his son truly was. He saw only the devastation in the room, the leaves and debris that been swept in from the storm, the blown-out plasma screen, the decimated bookshelf and me on the floor . . .

. . . and the photos of Jasmin Ahmadi that littered almost every flat surface, even the carpet at the chief of police's feet, where a few had fluttered out into the hallway when Jesse had opened the door.

He didn't yet understand what the photos meant, nor could he see—because no one could see it, no one but me and Jesse—the ghost of Mark Rodgers, still standing by the French doors, watching, waiting to see if justice really would be served, like I'd promised.

"What's happened?" Dr. Farhat asked, throwing a nervous glance at the table where the votive candles still stood. The only photo that still remained on the wall above them was the one of Zack and Jasmin in their Halloween costumes. The doctor seemed to be starting to put the clues together. "Why would this woman say that Zakaria killed Jasmin?"

"Because she's a lying bitch!" Zack screamed, trying to lunge at me. But Jesse's grip was too strong for him, and all he ended up doing was hurting himself. He did fling a few other choice swearwords at me, however, that caused his father to thunder at him, "Stop it! I will not have that kind of language in my house!"

Then Dr. Farhat turned to the mayor and chief of police and said, politely, "I apologize. I don't know what's come over my son. Maybe it's the storm. Or maybe . . . well, he's had a great shock. Truthfully, he's been acting this way ever since the death of his cousin—Jasmin Ahmadi. He's taken it—we've all taken it—very hard."

Mrs. Farhat was looking down at me, compassion—and resignation—in her beautiful dark eyes. "Are *you* all right, my dear?"

"Not really," I said. I didn't want to do it—especially to her, because she seemed so kind—but I had to. I'd promised Mark. And killing monsters is my job. "I took a wrong turn on the way to the bathroom, and your son and I ended up talking, and then all of a sudden, from out of nowhere, he flew into a homicidal rage and tried to kill me."

"I'm so sorry," Mrs. Farhat murmured, even as her son once again screamed that I was a liar.

But this time everyone ignored him. The chief prosecutor held out a hand and helped me to my feet. I could feel Jesse's worried gaze on me, so I tried not to lean too heavily on the tall man's grip, even though I wanted to. Instead, I leaned casually against the wall once he'd released my fingers, trying to appear as if I normally leaned against walls and was not in the least sore from the ass kicking I'd just received.

I could tell from Jesse's expression that he, at least, was not fooled.

"I thought about cancelling the party," Mrs. Farhat went on, her gaze downcast. "Perhaps I should have. But it's always so popular, and raises so much money for charity—"

"No need to apologize, ma'am," the chief of police said. "We understand." Having stooped to lift one of the photos of Jasmin, he now turned it over in his hand. It had become rain spattered, the edges torn from the battering it had received by the wind. "I can see the kids were very close."

"Well, yes," Dr. Farhat said, distractedly. He still seemed to be trying to make sense of what he was seeing and hearing, as if his youngest son was a heart he'd opened up on the operating table, only to find that it was diseased beyond repair. "As very young children. Not so close as they got older, of course, but—"

"That's your fault," Zack sneered. "Maybe if you'd been more strict with her—if her parents had, too—she'd have done what she was supposed to, and said yes to marrying me instead of that—"

He then said a word so foul, it caused every head in the room to turn sharply in his direction, particularly the chief prosecutor's, since he, along with Mark Rodgers, happened to belong to the race it slandered.

That's when Mrs. Farhat took two swift strides forward and slapped her son across the face. Now that the rain had stopped—and the party downstairs had gone strangely quiet, as well—the only ambient noise was the rhythmic pound of the ocean waves below, so the cracking sound the slap made was shockingly loud. It seemed to stun the people in the room more than the word Zack had used.

"How dare you?" Mrs. Farhat demanded, her dark eyes fiery with rage. "How dare you use that word in my house?"

"But it's true," Zack insisted, his own eyes shining—not because he was ashamed of himself, I knew, because he was incapable of shame. His tears were a mere physical reaction to the pain his mother had inflicted. "She was going to disgrace our family. She was going to humiliate us all—especially me. She was going to humiliate me. Can't you see that? Why can't any of you see that?"

The chief of police and chief prosecutor saw something, that's for sure. I know because of the sharp glance they exchanged. Then the chief of police cleared his throat.

"Um, excuse me, son," he said, with elaborate nonchalance. "Do you happen to remember where you were the night your cousin died?"

"With your wife," Zack replied with a sneer.

Mrs. Farhat buried her face in her hands. "Zakaria," she murmured. "Oh, Zakaria."

Dr. Farhat cleared his throat "My son is a fool, it's true. But there's no proof that he's a murderer."

"Actually, there is." Jesse's deep voice was gentle.

And before the boy could resist, Jesse pulled on one of the gold chains around Zack's neck, until the object hanging from it popped out from beneath his shirt collar.

It was a ring. A diamond solitaire on a gold band.

The prosecutor was across the room in a split second flat, holding the ring in his strong fingers.

"This is the engagement ring the Rodgers kid gave to the girl," he said, to no one in particular. He bent to examine it more closely, even as Zack squirmed to get away. But Jesse held on to him more tightly. "It's got their initials on the band exactly as the boy described. *MR and JA 4EVA.*"

Mark, who'd finally moved away from the French

doors toward the center of the room, mouthed the words along with him. Tears plainly glistened in his eyes behind the lenses of his glasses.

"I worked two jobs after school to pay for that ring," he said. "It cost two thousand dollars. But Jasmin is worth it." He choked a little. "*Was* worth it. Diamonds are supposed to be forever."

He broke down, weeping.

"I suppose you have a good explanation as to where you found that ring, kid," the police chief said, laying hold of Zack's arm and giving Jesse a nod to make it clear that he'd be taking over from here.

"Perhaps your wife gave it to him," quipped the prosecutor. "While they were in bed together the night of the accident."

"That would be some feat," the police chief said. "Seeing as how she was with me, watching the Lakers game."

"Don't worry, Zakaria," Dr. Farhat called, as his son was led away, struggling, by the two men. "We'll get you the best attorney money can buy."

Mrs. Farhat, dazed, only shook her head. Glancing at me before she left the room, she asked, almost as an afterthought, "Are you really all right?"

Jesse had crossed the room to slide an arm around me. I probably could have stood unaided, but it was nice to have a strong, masculine arm to lean on—especially one that was attached to such a tall, attractive body.

"I'm fine," I said, though this was an exaggeration. I was going to be sore tomorrow . . . even sorer than I was now.

Still, she was a nice lady, and she had enough to worry about.

"I'm glad," she said, and managed a smile that was at once both warm and regretful. "I'm so sorry about . . . about . . . well, about my son. I have another boy— Zakaria's older brother. He's away at university, like your friend." She glanced at Jesse, the smile turning into a beam. "We're very proud of him. Only he's studying to be a concert pianist. He's very talented." The smile faded. "Zakaria has always been a worry. And now . . ." The smile disappeared altogether. "Tell me . . . will you be pressing assault charges against my son? I'd understand it if you did. But I'd like . . . well, I'd like to be prepared."

"No," I said. "I won't be pressing any charges against your son, Mrs. Farhat."

She looked relieved . . . but only until I added, "But Mrs. Farhat, I think you do need to prepare for something else. Have you paid for any repairs on your son's truck recently? Has he had the paint touched up, or the bumper replaced? Things like that?"

"His truck . . ." A dark cloud—darker than any that had loomed outside during the storm—passed across her face, and I knew that she knew the truth now, beyond a shadow of a doubt. The ring was one thing—no one would ever be able to prove her son had coldly pulled that ring from Jasmin's finger as she lay dying in the wreckage of Mark's burning vehicle, though I hadn't the slightest doubt that's what had happened. Zack could claim he'd visited the site of the accident later, in his grief over his cousin's death, and found the ring lying on the side of the road.

But the repairs to his truck—which I'm sure the Farhats had unquestioningly paid for, as they did all their son's bills—were something else. They would never be able to dispute what those were for. Credit card charges for auto repairs, like diamonds, were forever.

And because of them, Mrs. Farhat would do her duty—not to her son, but to Jasmin—and make certain that Zack got what he deserved.

"God help us," she said. "Yes. Yes, I see. Thank you. I've got to be going now. You can show yourselves out. Have a good evening."

Then she was gone, leaving Jesse and me behind in her son's broken bedroom . . . with the ghost of the boy he'd killed, and who'd been trying all night to kill him in return.

Doce

"YOU DID IT," Mark said. "I didn't believe you when you said justice would be served. But you did it."

He was growing fainter by the second, the paranormal glow around him less and less bright. Part of that was because of the tremendous amount of psychic energy he'd exerted, summoning that storm.

But another, greater part was because he felt ready now. He felt ready to go wherever it was his soul was meant to be.

"I didn't do it," I said, wrapping an arm around Jesse's waist. "You did, Mark. Zack would never have admitted to any of it if it hadn't been for you scaring the living daylights out of him with that storm. The thing with the French doors? That was very excellently done for a BDP."

Mark looked confused. "What's BDP?"

"Beginner Deceased Person." I felt he'd earned the upgrade in title from Non-Compliant Deceased Person.

"Trust me, Mark," Jesse said. "You don't want to move past the beginner stage."

"He's right," I said. "Although you didn't do so badly yourself tonight, big guy." I gave Jesse a little squeeze. "You burst in at the perfect time."

"Timing has always been my forte," he admitted modestly.

"Everyone did pretty well tonight," I said. "Even our friends in law enforcement. Heck, even the media."

"I never thought I'd hear you utter those words," Jesse said, returning my squeeze with the supportive arm he'd slid around me.

"Well, they did hold back a description of the ring," I admitted. "Otherwise, Zack could have made a copy and been wearing that, and we'd never have been able to convince anyone what a psycho he is. I mean psycho in a thoroughly diagnostic way, of course, not pejoratively."

"Of course," Jesse said.

The ring. The ring. What was it about the ring that was bothering me—had *been* bothering me—so much?

"So I guess . . ." Mark had drifted toward the balcony. The temperature had already begun to rise, warming the night air. "I can just move on now, like you said."

"Well," I said, following him, gratified that Jesse hadn't released me. If I was lucky, he never would. "If there's nothing holding you back. I'm pretty sure Zack's not going to be putting any more flowers on Jasmin's grave, that's for sure. That prosecutor seemed to hate his guts, so I'm guessing he's probably going to charge him with everything in the book. What will probably happen is—"

"Mark?"

The voice, sweet as nectar, seemed to come from nowhere and everywhere all at once.

And then I saw her—just an amorphous glow, at first, like mist rising from the sea. Then she became more solid, the mist shifting into the shape of a beautiful slender girl—a girl I recognized, because I'd been looking at pictures of her all night.

Jasmin.

"Mark?" she said again, and smiled when she saw him. "Oh, Mark, there you are. I've been looking everywhere for you."

It didn't matter that she was floating twenty feet in the air, just off Zakaria Farhat's balcony. It didn't matter to Mark, anyway.

When she lifted her slender hand toward him, he raced to take it, floating as lightly as she was. You'd never think he was the same guy who, a few hours before, had very nearly killed me, first by unleashing a meteorological nightmare on me, then by swearing to kill his murderer, and causing that murderer to turn on me.

Well, I'd caused Zack to turn on me, I guess. But it had been in the name of justice.

Now Mark was in Jasmin's arms, softly murmuring her name, as she crooned his back. A moment later, there was a celestial burst of light—their two souls joining as one—and they both disappeared, together forever, into the afterlife.

"God," I said, when I was sure they were gone—and equally sure the tremble in my voice wouldn't betray the fact that I'd been weeping a little as I watched them. "I hate Valentine's Day."

"I know you do, *querida*." Jesse took my hand firmly in his own. If he suspected I'd been crying, it didn't show. "Let's go home."

We were driving past the beach—the one where he'd planned on proposing to me—when I finally realized what it was that had been bothering me about the ring.

"Stop the car!" I commanded.

He slammed on the brakes. "What is it? A cat? Did I hit it?"

"No, you didn't hit a cat. Pull over."

"Susannah, I can't pull over. Can't you see? It says no parking here. We'll get a ticket."

"Jesse, it's nearly midnight on the night of one of the biggest storms of the century. No one is around. We're not going to get a ticket. Just pull over."

He parked illegally, then followed me as I leaped from the car and ran to the steps that led down to the beach. "Susannah, I don't think this is a good idea. The tide is very high, and there's no moon. It's—"

"You have a penlight. Come on."

"How do you know I have a penlight?" He sounded bemused.

"Because you're a medical student. Hurry."

He was right about it being dark, of course, and about the tide being high. The waves were still agitated from Mark's storm, though the surf was dying down a little.

Still, there was only the tiniest slice of beach on which

to stand, and even then, the wind from the sea was more biting than bracing. There was no possible way to make a bonfire, because all of the driftwood was soaking wet from the rain, and of course we had no picnic basket, because we'd left it—and the sparkling wine—back in my dorm room at the Virgin Vault.

But we had privacy. There was no one else anywhere on the beach, because no one else was stupid enough to come near the bay in weather like this, in the middle of the night.

"Susannah," Jesse said, wrapping his arms around me as the wind whipped my long hair against us both. "What are we doing here? It was much warmer in the car."

"Aren't you glad you can feel cold, though?" I asked, hugging him back. "You used to not be able to. You used to not be able to feel cold, or hot, or anything."

"I could still feel, Susannah," he said, holding me closer. "Just emotions. Not the weather. Which actually there was something to be said for."

"Where did you get the ring?" I asked.

"What?"

"Where did you get the ring?" I shouted so that he could hear me above the pound of the surf. "Really? I know you said it was your mother's, and before that, it was your grandmother's. But Jesse, I know you came here with nothing. Nothing except the clothes on your back. I was with you. So where did you get the ring?"

He pushed me away from him—but not because he was angry, which was my first concern, but so that he could look down into my face in what meager light shone onto the beach from the streetlamps on Scenic Drive so high above our heads.

"Is *that* what upset you about my proposing?" he asked, the corners of his lips twisted upwards. "Where I got the ring?"

"I can't understand it," I said. "I thought we didn't have secrets from one another. Well, not real secrets." I had secrets, plenty of them, but only the kind that would hurt instead of help. I would take them to my grave— well, cremation urn—before I'd tell him about them. I didn't want him to turn into a murderer like Mark had almost been. "Where did you get it?"

"Oh, Susannah," he said, and pulled me close, then kissed the top of my head. "Why didn't you say so?"

"I'm saying so now. The only ring I know of you owning was the one you gave your last fiancée, Maria." I didn't like saying the name any more than Mark had liked saying Zack's. "But that was back in the 1800s, and you never got it back, because you ended up here . . . or murdered and a ghost, whichever parallel universe you care to believe is the right one. Unlike my stepbrother David, I don't really enjoy thinking about that kind of thing. Either way, you never ended up with your mother's precious ring."

"Ah," he said, and reached into the pocket of his jeans. "But I did. And do you want to know how I did?"

"Not really." I was feeling sick to my stomach. I wasn't sure if it was from the sight of the ring, having been rammed so hard in the gut by a murderous high school

boy, or not having eaten anything since lunch except radishes. "But I guess I asked."

"Father Dominic found it for sale on something called
eBay. There. Are you happy? Now will you marry me?"

I stared at him, aware that my mouth was probably
hanging open, but unable to close it. I couldn't do anything, really, but stare at him. "What?"

"EBay," Jesse repeated. "It's a website where people go
to buy and sell almost any—"

"I know what eBay is," I said. "I just . . . how did . . .
how could Father Dom have—"

"Apparently he goes on there a lot. Father Dominic is
very fond of the Internet. And he's been doing searches
in my name for some time, looking for items that might
have come from my family. He did one not long ago, and
the ring popped up. There was a letter with it, too, you
see, which is how he knew—"

"*Letter?* What letter?"

Now he began to look slightly uncomfortable. "It was
a letter from my mother to our local parish priest. As you
know, my family never knew what happened to me after
I . . . disappeared. According to this letter my mother refused to believe the rumors that I'd run off because I didn't
want to marry my cousin Maria and had instead gone to
seek my fortune in the Gold Rush. My father—well, I think
my father was more inclined to believe the worst of me."

I winced. Jesse's father had never supported his only
son's dream of becoming a physician. He'd wanted Jesse
to return from Carmel with Maria, his bride, and take
over the family ranch.

But that had never been going to happen in any universe.

"Oh, Jesse," I said. "I'm so sorry."

"It's all right, actually. My parents got the ring back—evidently there was some awkwardness over it, since Maria, too, believed she'd been stood up at the altar."

I winced again. I was the one responsible for Maria being stood up *twice*—once by Jesse, and then by the guy with whom she was two-timing Jesse. I'd be glad never to cross paths with *her* again.

"But she acquiesced in the end. And my mother ended up leaving the ring with our parish priest, along with the letter, saying that no matter what the reason for my disappearance, she forgave me. She wanted to make sure I knew that, Susannah. That's why she left the ring—and the letter—with the priest, and not my father or any of my sisters. She knew my father would burn the letter, or order my sisters to, as well, if he ever learned of them having it. But he could not order the priest to. The priest would keep it—and her secret—forever. And he did—at least until he, too, died, and the ring and letter passed down through many other priests who kept my mother's secret until at last the diocese folded. Then it must have fallen into the hands of whoever was trying to sell it online . . . and finally into those of one who knew what to do with it, Father Dominic."

I'd continued to keep my arms wrapped around his waist during the entirety of this speech. But now I simply couldn't stand it anymore. I dropped my arms and took a step away from him, allowing the cold wind to seep in between us.

"No, Jesse," I said. "No way that story is true. That is just too many coincidences. And you know I hate coincidences. They make no sense, and I hate things that don't make sense."

"I hate coincidences, too, Susannah." Jesse set his jaw, but wouldn't let me go. He reached out to grasp both my hands in his, the ring box hard as a stone in one of them against my fingers. "And I'm not particularly fond of miracles, either, except the one that brought you to me. But this isn't a coincidence, and it isn't a miracle, either. It makes perfect sense. And do you want to know why? My mother wrote about it in her letter. She said she knew someday I might lose faith in our family. She knew how much I disliked Maria, and didn't want to marry her, let alone be a rancher for a living instead of a doctor.

"But she also said that she knew the one thing I'd never lose faith in was the church. That's the other reason she left the ring—and the letter—with the priest. She said I may have stopped speaking to my family, but I'd never stop speaking to God, and that though I might never come home to her, I'd come back to the church someday. And when I did, I'd find her letter—and the ring. And she was right, Susannah. I never lost my faith. And through it, I met you."

My eyes stung. "Jesse," I said, though my throat was clogged suddenly with so much emotion I could hardly speak. "That's not—come on. That's not how this happened. I mean, *eBay*."

His grip on my fingers tightened. A dozen yards away, the Pacific kept up its rhythmic roar, and above us, the stars burned down in a night sky that was as cloudless as if Mark's storm for Jasmin had never happened at all.

"Let me finish," he said, his hands warm on mine. "After more than one hundred and fifty years of living alone in the darkness, I met you, Susannah, and through you, I met Father Dominic. Everything my mother said in her letter came true. It wasn't the same church, and it wasn't the same priest. But the letter and the ring were there, all because of you. And now I want to give that ring to you." He opened the ring box and dropped down to one knee before me in the sand. "So will you, Susannah Simon, kindly do me the honor of becoming my wife?"

Tears were streaming so thickly from my eyes that I could hardly see. The wind and salt spray whipping my hair across my face weren't helping much, either. I seemed to have picked the worst possible place in the world for a marriage proposal.

And yet, suddenly, I felt like the luckiest girl alive.

I sank down into the sand beside him.

"Yes, Jesse de Silva," I said, throwing my arms around his neck. "I will."

*You can take the boy out of the darkness. But
you can't take the darkness out of the boy.*

All Susannah Simon wants is to make a good
impression at her first job since graduating
from college (and since becoming engaged
to Dr. Jesse de Silva). But when she's hired as
a guidance counselor at her alma mater, she
stumbles across a decade-old murder, and soon
ancient history isn't all that's coming back to
haunt her. Old ghosts as well as new ones are
coming out of the woodwork, some to test
her, some to vex her, and it isn't only because
she's a mediator, gifted with second sight.

*What happens when old ghosts come
back to haunt you? If you're a mediator,
you might have to kick a little ass.*

From a sophomore haunted by the murderous
specter of a child, to ghosts of a very different
kind—including Paul Slater, Suze's ex, who shows
up to make a bargain Suze is certain must have
come from the Devil himself— Suze isn't sure
she'll make it through the semester, let alone to
her wedding night. Suze is used to striking first
and asking questions later. But what happens
when ghosts from her past—including one she
found nearly impossible to resist—strike first?

Uno

IT STARTED WHILE I was in the middle of an extremely heated online battle over a pair of black leather platform boots. That's when a chime sounded on my desktop, letting me know I'd received an e-mail.

Ordinarily I'd have ignored it, since my need for a pair of stylish yet functional boots was at an all-time high. My last ones had met with an unfortunate accident when I was mediating a particularly stubborn NCDP (Non-Compliant Deceased Person) down at the Carmel marina, and both of us had ended up in the water.

Unfortunately, I was at work, and my boss, Father Dominic, frowns on his employees ignoring e-mails at work, even at an unpaid internship like mine.

Muttering, "I'll be back," at the screen (in what I considered to be a pretty good imitation of Arnold Schwarzenegger as the Terminator), I clicked my in-box, keeping the screen to the auction open. With their steel-reinforced toes and chunky heels, these boots were perfect for dealing with those who needed a swift kick in the butt in order to encourage them to pass on to the afterlife, though I doubt that's why the person who kept trying to outbid me—Maximillian28, a totally lame screen name—wanted them so badly.

But if there's anything I've learned in the mediation business, it's that you shouldn't make assumptions.

Which is exactly what I realized when I saw the name of the e-mail's sender. It wasn't one of my coworkers at the Mission Academy, let alone a parent or a student. It wasn't a family member or friend, either.

It was someone I hadn't had any contact with in a long, long time—someone I'd hoped never to hear from again. Just seeing his name in my in-box caused my blood to boil . . . or freeze. I wasn't sure which.

Forgetting about the boots, I clicked on the e-mail's text.

To: suzesimon@missionacademy.edu
Fr: paulslater@slaterindustries.com
Re: Your House
Date: November 16 1:00:02 PM PST

Hi, Suze.
   I'm sure you've heard by now that my new company, Slater Industries, has purchased your old house on 99 Pine Crest Road, as well as the surrounding properties.
   You've never been a sentimental kind of girl, so I

*doubt you'll have a problem with the fact that we'll
be tearing your house down in order to make way for
a new Slater Properties development of moderately
sized family homes (see attached plans). My numbers
are below. Give me a call if you want to talk.*

*You know, it really bothers me that we haven't
stayed in touch over the years, especially since we were
once so close.*

> *Regards to Jesse.*
> *Best,*
> *Paul Slater*

> *P.S.: Don't tell me you're still upset over what
> happened graduation night. It was only a kiss.*

I stared at the screen, aware that my heart rate had
sped up. Sped up? I was so angry I wanted to ram my fist
into the monitor, as if by doing so I could somehow ram
it into Paul Slater's rock-hard abs. I'd hurt my knuckles
doing either, but I'd release a lot of pent-up aggression.

Did I *have a problem*, as Paul had so blithely put it,
with the fact that he'd purchased my old house—the
rambling Victorian home in the Carmel Hills that my
mom and stepdad had lovingly renovated nearly a decade
earlier for their new blended family (myself and my step-
brothers Jake, Brad, and David)—and was now intending
to tear it down in order to make way for some kind of
hideous subdivision?

Yeah. Yeah, I had *a problem* with that, all right, and with
nearly every other thing he'd written in his stupid e-mail.

And not because I'm sentimental, either.

He had the nerve to call what he'd done to me on graduation night "only a kiss"? Funny how all this time I'd been considering it something else entirely.

Fortunately for Paul, I'd never been stupid enough to mention it to my boyfriend, Jesse, because if I had, there'd have been a murder.

But since Hispanic males make up about 37 percent of the total prison population in California (and Paul evidently had enough money to buy the entire street on which I used to live), I didn't see a real strong chance of Jesse getting off on justifiable homicide, though that's what Paul's murder would have been, in my opinion.

Without stopping to think—huge mistake—I pulled my cell phone from the back pocket of my jeans and angrily punched in one of the numbers Paul had listed. It rang only once before I heard his voice—deeper than I remembered—intone smoothly, "This is Paul Slater."

"What the hell is your problem?"

"Why, Susannah Simon," he said, sounding pleased. "How nice to hear from you. You haven't changed a bit. Still so ladylike and refined."

"Shut the hell up."

I'd like to point out that I didn't say *hell* either time. There's a swear jar on my desk—Father Dominic put it there due to my tendency to curse. I'm supposed to stick a dollar in it for every four-letter word I utter, five dollars for every F-bomb I drop.

But since there was no one in the office to overhear me, I let the strongest weapons in my verbal arsenal fly freely. Part of my duties in the administrative offices of the Junípero Serra Mission Academy (grades K–12)—where I'm currently trying to earn some of the practicum credits I need to get my certification as a school counselor—are to answer the phone and check e-mails while all of my supervisors are at lunch.

What do my duties not include? Swearing. Or making personal phone calls to my enemies.

"I just wanted to find out where you are," I said, "so I can drive to that location and then slowly dismember you, something I obviously should have done the day we met."

"Same old Suze," Paul said fondly. "How long has it been, anyway, six years? Almost that. I don't think I've heard from you since the night of our high-school graduation, when your stepbrother Brad got so incredibly drunk on Goldschläger that he hurled all over Kelly Prescott's Louboutins. Ah, memories."

"He wasn't the only one who was drunk, if I recall," I reminded him. "And that isn't all that happened that night. You know what I've been doing since then, besides getting my counseling degree? Working out, so that when we meet again, I can—"

I launched into a highly anatomical description of just where, precisely, I intended to insert Paul's head after I physically removed it from his body.

"Suze, Suze, Suze." Paul feigned shock. "So much hostility. I find it hard to believe they allowed someone like you into a counseling training program. Have the people in charge there ever even *met* you?"

"If they met you, they'd be wondering the same thing I am: how a manipulative freak like you isn't locked up in a maximum-security penitentiary."

"What can I say, Simon? You've always brought out the romantic in me."

"I think you're confusing the word *romantic* with sociopathic sleazebag. And you're lucky it was Debbie Mancuso and not Jesse who came along when you were pawing at me that night like an oversexed howler monkey, because if it had been, he'd—"

"—have given me another one of those trademarked beatings of his that I so richly deserve. Yes, yes, I know, Suze, I've heard all this before."

Paul sighed. He and my boyfriend have never gotten along, mainly because Jesse had been an NCDP for a while and Paul—who, like me, was born with the so-called "gift" to communicate with those trapped in the spirit world—had been determined to keep him that way, mostly so that Paul could get into my pants.

Fortunately, he'd failed on both accounts.

"Could we move on, please?" Paul asked. "This is very entertaining, but I want to get to the part about how I now own your family home. You heard the news, right? Not about your house—I can tell by your less than graceful reaction that you only just found out about that. I mean about how Gramps finally croaked, and left me the family fortune?"

"Oh, no. Paul, I'm—"

I bit my lip. His grandfather had been cantankerous at times, but he'd also been the only person in Paul's family—besides his little brother, Jack—who'd genuinely seemed to care about him. I wasn't surprised to hear that he'd passed on, however. The old man had already been in pretty bad shape when I'd met him from "shifting" back and forth too often through time, a skill mediators possess, but are warned not to use. It's considered hazardous to their health.

Still, it felt wrong to say *I'm sorry for your loss* to Paul, considering he was acting like the world's biggest jackhole.

It didn't end up mattering. Paul wanted something from me, but it wasn't my condolences.

"Yeah, you're talking to one of *Los Angeles* magazine's most eligible bachelors," he went on, oblivious. "Of course my parents aren't too happy about it. They had the nerve to take me to court to contest the will, can you believe that?"

"Uh . . . yes?"

"Funny. But justice prevailed, and I'm now the president and CEO of Slater Industries. I've got a home on both coasts and a private jet to fly between them, but—as the magazine put it—no one special with whom to share them." I could hear the mocking tone in his voice. "Interested in being that special someone, Suze?"

"I'll pass, thanks," I said coolly. "Especially since you can't think of anything more creative to do with your new fortune than knock down other people's houses. Which I don't think you can even do legally. Mine's nearly two hundred years old. It's still got the original carved newel post on the staircase from when it was built in 1850. It has stained-glass windows. It's a historic landmark."

"Actually, it isn't. Oh, it's quaintly charming in its own way, I suppose, but nothing historic ever occurred there. Well, except for what happened between you and me," he smirked, "and considering the way you've been avoiding me these past few years, I guess I'm not the only one who remembers that as being historically significant."

"Nothing ever happened between us, Paul," I said. He was only trying to get under my skin, the same way he'd tried to get under my bra at graduation. That's how he operated, much like a chigger, or various other bloodsucking parasites. "Nothing good, anyway."

"Ouch, Simon! You sure know how to hurt a guy. I distinctly recall one afternoon in my bedroom when you did not seem at all repulsed by my advances. Why, you even—"

"—walked out on you, remember? And no one can tear down a house that old. That has to be a violation of some kind of city code."

"You slip enough money to the right politicians, Simon, you can get permits to do anything you want in the great state of California. That's why they call it the land of opportunity. Congratulations, by the way, on your stepfather's success. Who would have thought that little home-improvement show of Andy Ackerman's would become an international sensation. Where'd your parents move to with all the money he's raking in from the syndication rights? Bel Air? Or the Hills? Don't worry, it happens to everyone. I'm sure they haven't let fame go to their heads. Your mother is a lovely woman with such gracious manners, which is more than I can say for her only daughter—"

"You say one more word about my mother," I snarled, "and I will end you, Paul, like I should have done years ago. I will find you, wherever you are, remove your head from your body, and stuff it up your—"

"You already used that one," Paul reminded me. "So I take it that you *do* have a sentimental side, Suze. How surprising. I always knew you had a soft spot for that undead boyfriend of yours, of course, but I never expected it to extend to real estate. Oh, wait—Jesse must be more than just a boyfriend now that you managed to reunite his body with his soul. I'm afraid I've been a bit out of the loop lately—and who has time to read their alumni newsletter anyway? Have you two tied the knot? Wait, silly me—of *course* you have. It's been six years since high school! I know a love as passionate as the one you and that necromantic cholo shared couldn't *possibly* wait six years to be consummated. And from what I remember, Hector 'Jesse' de Silva respected you far too much ever to try to get into your pants without the sanctity of holy matrimony."

I felt my cheeks begin to burn. I told myself it was indignation at his racism—*necromantic cholo*? Really?— but I knew some of it was due to a different emotion entirely. I was happy Paul wasn't in the same room with me, or he'd surely have noticed. He'd always been discomfortingly sharp-eyed.

"Jesse and I are engaged," I said, controlling— with an effort—my impulse to swear at him some more. In the past, anytime Paul was able to evoke any kind of emotion from me at all—even a negative one—it pleased him.

And the last thing I'd ever wanted to do was please Paul Slater.

"Engaged?" Paul crowed. "What is this, the 1950s? People still get *engaged*? Do people even get *married*? I mean, straight people?"

I really should have thought before I acted and never called him in the first place, I thought miserably, eyeing a poster Ms. Diaz, the Mission Academy guidance counselor, had stuck on the wall over by the entrance to her office. It was one of those posters ubiquitous to the profession, a blown-up photo of a kitten struggling to hang on to a tree branch emblazoned with the words *Aim High*!

Too late, I realized I ought to have aimed high and approached Paul with cool dispassion, not let my emotions get in the way. That was the only way to handle him.

But he'd always been good at pushing my buttons.

All my buttons.

"Isn't an engagement a little old-school for a modern girl like you, Simon?" he went on. "Oh, wait, I forgot . . . Walking Dead Boy likes to do things the old-school way, doesn't he? Does that mean"—he sounded more pleased with himself than ever—"you two are *waiting for marriage*?"

I felt another overwhelming urge to lash out and punch something, anything, maybe even the tabby kitten in the poster. But the wall behind it was three feet thick, built in the 1700s, and had withstood many a Northern California earthquake. It would definitely withstand my fist.

"That is none of your business," I said, so icily that I

was surprised the phone in my hand didn't freeze to my face.

I was trying hard not to clue Paul in to how annoyed I was with my boyfriend's prehistoric notion that we not only couldn't marry until he was in a financial position to support me and whatever children we might have (even though I'd assured him I was on the pill and planned to stay on it until I'd finished my MA and had a job with full dental, at least), we couldn't move in together.

Even worse, Jesse insisted we had to wait until we'd formally exchanged vows—in a church, with him in a suit, and me in a white dress and veil, no less—before we could enjoy conjugal relations. It was the least he could do, he insisted, out of "respect" for all that I had done for him, not only bringing him back to life, but providing him with a life worth living.

I'd let him know many, many times, and in no uncertain terms, that I could live without that kind of respect.

But what else could you expect from a guy who'd been born during the reign of Queen Victoria? Not to mention murdered in—then buried behind, then spent 150 years haunting—the very same house Paul was threatening to tear down?

This had to have something to do with *why* Paul was tearing it down. I'd always suspected Paul of being jealous that in the end I'd chosen the ghost instead of him.

But how could I not? Even in the days when Jesse hadn't had a pulse, he'd had more heart than Paul.

"Waiting for marriage," Paul repeated. He was hooting with laughter that bordered on tears. "Oh, God. That is so sweet: It really is, Simon. I think your stepdad's TV show is about the wrong person. They should be filming you and that boyfriend of yours, and call it *The Last Virgins*. I swear it'd be the highest-rated show since *Ghost Mediator*."

"Go ahead," I said, lifting my heels to my desk and crossing my feet at the ankles. "Laugh it up, Paul. You know what Jesse's doing right now? His medical residency."

That hit home. Paul abruptly stopped laughing.

"That's right," I went on, beginning to enjoy myself. "While you've been out being named one of LA's most eligible bachelors for doing nothing but inheriting your grandfather's money, Jesse passed the MCATs with one of the highest scores in California state history and got a medical degree at UCSF. Now he's doing a pediatrics fellowship at St. Francis Medical Center in Monterey. He just has to finish up his residency there, and he'll be fully licensed to practice medicine. Do you know what that means?"

Paul's voice lost some of its laughter. "He stole someone else's identity? Because that's the only way I can see someone who used to be a walking corpse getting into UCSF. Except as a practice cadaver, of course."

"Jesse was born in California, you idiot."

"Yeah, before it became a state."

"What it means," I went on, tipping back in my chair, "is that next year, after Jesse's board-certified, and I've gotten my certification, we'll be getting married."

At least, if everything went according to schedule,

and Jesse won the private grant he'd applied for to open his own practice. I didn't see the point in mentioning any of these "if's" to Paul . . . or that I didn't know how much longer I could go on swimming laps in the dinky pool in the courtyard of my apartment building, trying to work out my frustration about my fiancé and his very nineteenth-century views about love, honor, and sex . . . views I'm determined to respect as much as he (unfortunately) respects my body.

Things have gotten steamy between us enough times for me to know that what's behind the front of those tight jeans of Jesse's will be worth the wait, though. Our wedding night is going to be *epic*.

Unless one of those many "if's" doesn't work out, or something happens to get the groom thrown in jail. Of all the obstacles I'd envisioned getting in the way of our very much deserved wedding night, Paul popping around again was the last thing I'd expected.

"But more important, it means someday we'll be opening our own practice, specializing in helping sick kids," I went on. "Not that helping other people is a concept I'd expect *you* to understand."

"That's not true," Paul said. There was no laughter in his voice at all now. "I've always wanted to help you, Suze."

"Is that what you call what you did to me graduation night, when you said you had a present you had to give to me in private, so I followed you outside and you threw me up against the mission wall and shoved your hand up my skirt?" I asked him, acidly. "You consider that *helping* me?"

"I do," he said. "I was trying to help teach you not to waste your time on formerly deceased Latino do-gooders who consider it a sin to get nasty without a marriage license."

"Well," I said, lowering my feet from my desktop. "I'm hanging up now. It was not at all a pleasure speaking to you again after all these years, Paul. Please die slowly and painfully. Buh-bye."

"Wait," Paul said urgently before I could press End. "Don't go. I wanted to say—"

"What? That you won't tear down my house if I take lessons from you in how to be a more effective mediator? Sorry, Paul, that might have worked when I was sixteen, but I'm too old to fall for that one again."

He sounded offended. "The thing with your house is just business. I only told you about it as a courtesy. What I wanted to say is that I'm sorry."

Paul Slater had never apologized for anything before . . . and meant it. He caught me off guard.

"Sorry for what?"

"Sorry for what I said about Jesse just now, and sorry for what happened that night. You're right, Suze, I'd had way too much to drink. I know that's no excuse, but it's the truth. Honestly, I barely remember what happened."

Was he kidding? "Let me remind you. After you tried to nail me against that wall, I gave *you* a present. It was with my knee, to your groinal area. Does that refresh your memory?"

"A man doesn't forget that kind of pain, Simon. But

what happened after that is a bit hazy. Is that when Debbie Mancuso came along?"

"It was. She seemed eager to tend to the wound I gave you."

"Then you should be the one apologizing to me. Debbie's ministrations were far from tender. She straddled me like she thought I was a damned gigolo—"

"Watch it," I growled. "Debbie's married to my stepbrother Brad now. And obviously I didn't knee you nearly as hard as I should have if you were still able to get it on with Debbie afterward. The last thing you're ever going to hear from me is an apology."

"Then accept mine, and let me make it up to you. I have a proposal."

I barked with laughter. "Oh, right!"

"Simon, I'm serious."

"That'll be a first."

"It could save your home."

I stopped laughing. "I'm listening. Maybe."

"Give me another chance."

"I said I'm listening."

"No, that's the proposal. Give me another chance."

Dos

THE SCHOOL OFFICE was air-conditioned, but the shiver I felt down my spine had nothing to do with the fact that my supervisors (some of whom dress in religious habit) liked to keep the thermostat at a crisp sixty-five degrees.

"I'm sorry," I said, glad the shiver didn't show in my voice. "I'm actually very busy and important and don't have time for rich jerks from my past who want to make amends. But I wish you luck on your path toward transformative enlightenment. Bye now."

"Suze, wait. Don't you want to save your house?"

"It isn't mine anymore, remember? It's yours. So I don't care what happens to it."

"Come on, Suze. This is the first time in six years you've actually called me back when I've reached out to you. I know you care—about the house."

He was right. I'd been upset when Mom told me she

and my stepdad, Andy, were selling it—much more upset than Jesse when he heard the news.

"It's only a house, Susannah," he'd said. "Your parents haven't lived there in years, and neither have we. It has nothing to do with us."

"How can you say that?" I'd cried. "That house has everything to do with us. If it weren't for that house, we'd never have found one another!"

He'd laughed. "Maybe, *querida*. Then again, maybe not. I have a feeling I'd have found you, and you me, no matter where we were. That house is only a place, and not our place, not anymore. Our place is together, wherever we happen to be."

Then he'd pulled me close and kissed me. It had been hard to feel bad about anything after that.

I guess I could understand why the big, rambling Victorian on 99 Pine Crest Road meant nothing to him. To Jesse, it's the house in which he was killed.

To me, however, it was the house in which we'd met and slowly, over time and through many misunderstandings, fell in love—though it had seemed for years like a doomed romance: he was a Non-Compliant Deceased Person. I was a girl whose job it was to rid the world of his kind. It had ended up working out, but barely.

While the so-called "gift" of communicating with the dead might sound nifty, believe me, when a ghost shows up in your bedroom—even one who looks as good with his shirt off as Jesse does—the reality isn't at all the way they portray it in the movies or on TV or the stupid new hit reality show *Ghost Mediator* (which is, I'm sorry to say, based on a best-selling video and role-playing game of the same name).

The "reality" is heartbreaking and sometimes quite violent . . . as my need for new boots illustrated.

Except, of course, that in the end it was my "gift" that had enabled me to meet and get to know Jesse, and even help return his soul to his corporal self, though my boss and fellow mediator, Mission Academy principal Father Dominic, likes to think that was "a miracle" we should be grateful for. I'm still on the fence about whether or not I believe in miracles. There's a rational and scientific explanation for everything. Even the "gift" of seeing ghosts seems to have a genetic component. There's probably a scientific explanation for what happened with Jesse, too.

One thing there's no explanation for—at least that I've found so far—is Paul. Even though he's the one who showed me the nifty time-jumping trick that eventually led to the "miracle" that brought Jesse back to the living from the dead, Paul didn't do it out of the goodness of his heart. He did it out of a desire to get in my pants.

"Look, Paul," I said. "You're right. I do care. But about people, not houses. So why don't you take your amends and your fancy new housing development and your private jet and stick them all up your external urethral orifice, which in case you don't know is the medical term for dick hole. Adios, muchacho."

I started to hang up until the sound of Paul's laughter stopped me.

"Dick hole," he repeated. "Really, Simon?"

I couldn't help placing the phone to my ear again. "Yes, really. I'm highly educated in the correct medical terms for sexual organs now, since I'm engaged to a doctor. And that isn't just where you can stick your amends, by the way, it's also what you are."

"Fine. But what about Jesse?"

"What *about* Jesse?"

"I could see you not caring about me, or about the house, but I think you'd be at least a little concerned about your boyfriend."

"I am, but I fail to see what your tearing down my house has to do with him."

"Only everything. Are you telling me you really don't remember all those Egyptian funerary texts of Gramps' that we used to study together after school? That hurts, Suze. That really hurts. Two mixed-up mediators, poring over ancient hieroglyphics . . . I thought we had something special."

When you're a regular girl and a guy is horny for you, he invites you over to his house after school to watch videos.

When you're a mediator, he invites you over to study his grandfather's ancient Egyptian funerary texts, so you can learn more about your calling.

Yeah. I was real popular in high school.

"What about them?" I demanded.

"Oh, not much. I just thought you'd remember what the *Book of the Dead* said about what happens when a dwelling place that was once haunted is demolished . . . how a demon disturbed from its final resting place will unleash the wrath of eternal hellfire upon all it encounters, cursing even those it once held dear with the rage of a thousand suns. That kind of thing."

I swore—but silently, to myself.

Paul's grandfather, in addition to being absurdly wealthy, had also been one of the world's most preeminent Egyptologists. When it came to obscure, ancient curses written on crumbling pieces of papyrus, the guy was top of his field.

That's why I was swearing. I'd been wrong: Paul wasn't calling to make amends. This was something way, way worse.

"Nice try, Paul," I said, attempting to keep my voice light and my heart rate steady. "Except I'm pretty sure that one was about mummies buried in pyramids, not ghosts who once haunted residential homes in Northern California. And while Jesse was never exactly an angel, he was no demon, either."

"Maybe not to you. But he treated me like—"

"Because you were always trying to exorcise him out of existence. That would make anyone feel resentful. And 99 Pine Crest Road wasn't his final resting place. Even before he became alive again, we found his remains and moved them."

I couldn't see Jesse's headstone from my desk, but I knew it was sitting only a few dozen yards away, in the oldest part of the mission cemetery. On holy days of obligation, it's the fifth graders' job to leave carnations on it (as they do all the historic gravestones in the cemetery), as well as pull any weeds that might have sprouted from it.

The fact that there's nothing buried under Jesse's grave—since he happens to be alive and well—is something I don't see any reason to let the fifth graders know. Kids benefit from being outdoors. Too much time playing video games has been shown to slow their social skills.

"So tearing down the place where he died isn't going to hurt him," I went on. "I'm not personally a fan of subdivisions, but hey, if that's what floats your boat, go for it. Anything else? I really do have to go now, I've got a ton of things to do to get ready for the wedding."

Paul laughed. Apparently my officious tone hadn't fooled him.

"Oh, Suze. I love how so much in the world has changed, but not you. That boyfriend of yours haunted that crummy old house forever, waiting around for . . . just what *was* he waiting for, anyway? Murder victims are the most stubborn of all spooks to get rid of." He said the word *spooks* the way someone in a detergent commercial would say the word *stains*. "All they want is justice—or, as in Jesse's case, revenge."

"That isn't true," I made the mistake of interrupting, and got rewarded by more of Paul's derisive laughter.

"Oh, isn't it? What was it you think he was waiting around for all those years, then, Suze? You?"

I felt my cheeks heat up again. "No."

"Of course you do. But that love story of yours may not have such a happy ending after all."

"Really, Paul? And why is that? Because of something written on a two-thousand-year-old papyrus scroll? I think you've been watching too many episodes of *Ghost Mediator*."

His voice went cold. "I'm just telling you what the curse says—that restoring a soul to the body it once inhabited is a practice best left to the gods."

"What are you even talking about? *You're* the one who—"

"Suze, I only did what people like you and me are supposed to—attempt to help an unhappy soul pass on to his just rewards."

"By sneaking back through time to keep him from dying in the first place so I'd never meet him?"

"Never mind what I did. Let's talk about what *you* did. The curse goes on to say that any human who attempts to resurrect a corpse will be the first to suffer its wrath when the demon inside it is woken."

"Well, that's ridiculous, since there's no demon inside Jesse, and I didn't resurrect him. It was a miracle. Ask Father Dom."

"Really, Suze? Since when did you start believing in miracles?" I hated that he knew me so well. "And when did you start believing that you could tinker around with space and time—and life and death—without having to pay the consequences? If you help to create a monster, you should be prepared for that monster to come back and bite you in the ass. Or are you completely unfamiliar with the entire Hollywood horror movie industry?"

"Fiction," I said, my mouth dry. "Horror movies are fiction."

"And the concept of good and evil? Is that fiction? Think about it, Simon. You can't have one without the other. There has to be a balance. You got your good. Ghost Boy's alive now, and giving back to the community with his healing hands . . . which makes me want to puke, by the way. But where's the bad? Have you not noticed there's something missing from this little miracle of yours?"

"Um," I said, struggling to come up with a flippant reply.

Because he was right. As any Californian worth his flip-flops could tell you, you can't have yin without yang, surf without sand, a latte without soy (because no one in California drinks full dairy, except for me, but I was born in New York City).

"I assume the bad is . . . you." This was weak, but it was the best I could come up with, given the feeling of foreboding slowly creeping up my spine.

"Very funny, Suze. But you're going to have to come up with something better. Humor doesn't work as a defense against the forces of evil. Which are dwelling, as you very well know, inside your so-called miracle boy, just waiting for the chance to lash out and kill you and everyone you love for what you did."

Now he'd gone too far. "I do *not* know that. How do *you* know that? You haven't even seen him in six years. You don't know anything about us. You can't just come here and—"

"I don't *have* to have seen him to know that he didn't escape from having lived as a spook for a century and a half without having brushed up against some pretty malevolent shit. De Silva didn't just walk through the valley of the shadow of death, Simon. He set up camp and toasted marshmallows there. No one can come out of something like that unscathed, however many kids he's curing of cancer now, or however many wedding-gift registries his girlfriend's signing up for in order to assure herself that everything's just fine and dandy."

"That's not fair," I protested. "And that's not fair. You might as well be saying that anyone who's ever suffered from any trauma is destined never to overcome it, no matter how hard they try."

"Really? You're going to fall back on grad school psychobabble?" His voice dripped with amusement. "I expected better from you. Can you honestly tell me, Simon, that when you look into de Silva's big brown telenovela eyes, you never see any shadows there?"

"No. No, of course I do, sometimes, because he's human, and human beings aren't happy one hundred percent of the time."

"Those aren't the kind of shadows I'm talking about, and you know it."

I realized I was squeezing my phone so hard an ugly red impression of its hard plastic casing had sunk into my skin. I had to switch hands.

Because he was right. I did see occasional glimpses of darkness in Jesse's eyes . . . and not sadness, either.

And while I hadn't been lying when I'd told Paul about

Jesse's desire to help heal the sick and most downtrodden of our society—it was an integral part of his personality—I did worry sometimes that the reason Jesse fought so desperately against death when he saw it coming for his weakest patients was that he feared it was also coming back for him . . .

Or, worse, that there was still a part of it inside him.

If what the *Book of the Dead* said was true, and Paul really did tear down 99 Pine Crest Road, there was no telling what that destruction might unleash.

And it didn't seem likely we could count on yet another miracle to save us. A person is only given so many miracles in a lifetime, and it felt like Jesse and I had received more than our fair share.

If miracles even exist. Which I'm not saying they do.

As if he'd once again sensed what I was thinking, Paul chuckled. "See what I mean, Simon? You can take the boy out of the darkness, but you can't take the darkness out of the boy."

"Fine," I said. "What do you want from me, exactly, in order to keep you from tearing down my house and releasing the Curse of the Papyrus, or whatever it is? Forgiveness? Great. I forgive you. Will you go now and leave me alone?"

"No, but thanks for the offer," Paul said, smooth as silk. "And it's called the Curse of the Dead. There's no such thing as the Curse of the Papyrus. Curses are written on papyrus. They're not—"

"Just tell me what you want, Paul."

"I told you what I want. Another chance."

"You're going to have to elaborate. Another chance at what?"

"You. One night. If I can't win you over from de Silva in one night, I'm not worthy of the name Slater."

"You have got to be kidding me."

If I hadn't felt so sick to my stomach, I'd have laughed. I tried not to let my conflicting feelings—scorn, fear, confusion—show in my voice. Paul fed off feelings the way black holes fed off stars.

"I'm not, actually," he said. "I told you, it's never a good idea to joke when the forces of evil are involved."

"Paul. First of all, you can't win back something you never had."

"Suze, where is this coming from? I really thought you and I had something once. Are you honestly trying to tell me it was all in my head? Because I've had a lot of time to think it over, and I have to say, I don't agree."

"Second of all, I'm engaged. That means I'm off the market. And even if I wasn't, threatening to tear down a multimillion-dollar house and release some kind of evil spirit that may or may not live inside my boyfriend is beneath even—"

He cut me off. "What do I care if you're engaged? If Hec*tor* doesn't put enough value on your relationship to bother consummating it"—Paul put an unpleasantly rolled trill on the second syllable of Jesse's given name—"which I know he doesn't, you're still fair game as far as I'm concerned."

"Wait." I could hardly believe my ears. "That isn't fair. Jesse's Roman Catholic. Those are his *beliefs*."

"And you and I are non-believers," Paul pointed out. "So I don't understand why you'd want to be with a guy who believes that—"

"I never said I was a non-believer. I believe in *facts*. And the fact is, I want to be with Jesse because he makes me feel like a better person than I suspect I actually am."

There was a momentary silence from the other end of the phone. For a second or two I thought I might actually have gotten through to him, made him see that what he was doing was wrong. Paul did have some goodness in him—I knew, because I'd seen it in action once or twice. Even complete monsters can have one or two likable characteristics. Hitler liked dogs, for instance.

But unfortunately the good part of Paul was buried beneath so much narcissism and greed, it hardly ever got a chance to show itself, and now was no exception.

"Wow, Simon, that was a real Hallmark moment," he snarked. "You know I could make you feel good—"

"Well, you've gotten off to an excellent start by threatening to turn my fiancé into a demon."

"Don't shoot the messenger, baby. I'm not the bad guy here. If I weren't the one tearing down your house, it was going to be some other filthy-rich real-estate developer."

"I highly doubt that."

"What the hell, Simon? You should be grateful to me. I'm trying to do you a solid. Where is all this hostility coming from?"

"My heart."

"This is bullshit." Now Paul sounded pissed off. "Why should I have to respect some other guy's beliefs? It's called free enterprise. Since when can't a man try to win something that's still on the open market?"

"Did we just travel back through time again to the year 1850? Are women something you believe you can actually *own*?"

"Funny. I'll give you that, you've always been funny, Simon. That's the thing I've always liked best about you. Well, that, and your ass. You still have a great ass, don't you? I tried to look up photos of you on social media, but you keep a surprisingly low profile. Oh, shit, wait, never mind. You're a feminist, right? You probably think that ass remark was sexist."

"*That's* what you're worried about? That I'm going to think you're sexist? Not that I'm going to report you to the cops for trying to blackmail me into going out with you?"

"I'm afraid you're going to find any wrongdoing on my part a little difficult to prove to the cops, Suze, even if you've been recording this phone call, which I'm guessing you only thought of doing just now. No monetary sums have been mentioned, and even if you call it coercion, I'm pretty sure you're going to have a hard time explaining to the cops exactly how my tearing down a property I legally own is threatening you. Though if you mention the stuff about the ancient Egyptian funerary texts, it will probably give the po-po a good laugh."

Unfortunately, he was right. That was the part that burned the most. Until he added, "Oh, and I'm going to expect a little more than you merely *going out* with me. Not to be crude, but virtue is hardly something *I* value.

Unlike Hector, I'm not particularly marriage minded. But I guess being married to you might be fun . . . like being a storm chaser. You'd never know what to expect from day to day. But I'm getting ahead of myself. First, our date—it will definitely have to include physical intimacy. Otherwise, how else will I be able to show you I've changed?"

I was so stunned, I was temporarily unable to form a reply, even a four-letter one, which for me was unusual.

"Don't worry," he said soothingly. "It's been a long time since I've touched Goldschläger. I've vastly improved my technique. I won't throw you against another wall."

"Wow," I said, when I could finally bring myself to speak. "What *happened* to you? When did you become so hard up for female company that you had to resort to sextortion? Have you ever thought of trying Tinder?"

He laughed. "Good one! See, I've missed this. I've missed us."

"There was never any us, you perv. What happened between you and Kelly, anyway?"

"Kelly?" Paul hooted some more. "Kelly *Prescott*? I guess you haven't been reading the online alumni newsletters, either."

"No," I admitted guiltily. The guilt was only because my best friend, CeeCee, wrote the newsletter for our graduating class, and I paid no attention to it.

"Well, let's just say Kelly and I weren't exactly meant for each other—not like you and me. But don't worry about old Kel. She's rebounded with some guy twice her age, but with twice as much money as I have—which is saying a lot, because as I mentioned, I'm flush. Kelly Prescott became Mrs. Kelly . . . Walters, I think is what it said on the announcement. She had some huge reception at the Pebble Beach resort. What, you weren't invited?"

"I don't recall. My social calendar's pretty full these days."

I was lying, of course. I'd been invited to Kelly's wedding, but only because I'm related through marriage to her best friend Debbie, who'd been the maid of honor. I'd politely declined, citing a (fake) prior commitment, and no one had mentioned missing me.

Weddings aren't really my thing, anyway. Large gatherings of the living tend to attract the attention of the undead, and I usually end up having to mediate NCDPs between swallows of beer.

My own wedding is going to be different. I'll kick the butt of any deadhead who shows up there uninvited.

"So when are we having dinner?" Paul asked. "Or, more to the point, what comes after dinner. And I'm not talking about dessert."

"When Jupiter aligns with planet Go Screw Yourself."

"Aw, Suze. Your sexy pillow talk is what I've missed most about you. I'll be in Carmel this weekend. I'll text you the deets about where to meet up then. But really, it doesn't sound like you're taking anything I've just told you about the potential threat to your boyfriend's life very seriously."

"I do take it seriously. Seriously enough to be looking forward to seeing you as it will allow me to fulfill my long-held dream of sticking my foot up your ass."

"You can put any body part of yours in any orifice of mine you please, Simon, so long as I get to do the same to you."

I was so angry I suggested that he suck a piece of anatomy I technically don't possess, since I'm female.

It was unfortunate that Sister Ernestine, the vice-principal, chose that particular moment to return from lunch.

"*What* did you say, Susannah?" she demanded.

"Nothing." I hung up on Paul and stuffed my phone back into the pocket of my jeans. I was going to have to deal with him—and whether or not there was any truth to this "curse" he was talking about—at another time. "How was lunch, Sister?"

"We'll discuss how much you owe the swear jar later, young lady. We have bigger problems at the moment."

Did we ever. I figured that out as soon as I saw the dead girl behind her.

About the Author

MEG CABOT WAS born in Bloomington, Indiana. In addition to her adult contemporary fiction she is the author of the best-selling young adult fiction series The Princess Diaries. Over twenty-five million copies of her novels for children and adults have sold worldwide. Meg lives in Key West, Florida, with her husband.

Discover great authors, exclusive offers, and more at hc.com